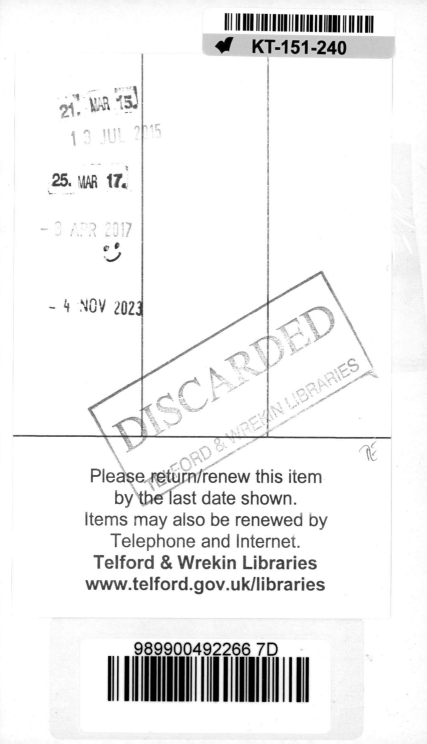

Also by Jonathan Smith

FICTION

Wilfred and Eileen
The English Lover
In Flight
Come Back
Summer in February
Night Windows

NON-FICTION

Good Enough? (with Chris Cowdrey)
The Learning Game
The Following Game

THE CHURCHILL SECRET
KBO

JONATHAN SMITH

Little, Brown

LITTLE, BROWN

First published in Great Britain in 2015 by Little, Brown

1 3 5 7 9 10 8 6 4 2

All characters and events in this publication, other than those clearly in the public domain, are fictitious and any resemblance to real persons, living or dead, is purely coincidental.

A CIP catalogue record for this book is available from the British Library.

ISBN 978-0-349-14025-4

Typeset in Baskerville by M Rules
Printed and bound in Great Britain by
Clays Ltd, St Ives plc

Papers used by Little, Brown are from well-managed forests and other responsible sources.

FSC
www.fsc.org
MIX
Paper from
responsible sources
FSC® C104740

Little, Brown
An imprint of
Little, Brown Book Group
100 Victoria Embankment
London EC4Y 0DY

An Hachette UK Company
www.hachette.co.uk

www.littlebrown.co.uk

for Jeremy Cowdrey

Keep right on to the end of the road,
Keep right on to the end.
Though the road may be long, let your heart be strong,
Keep right on to the end.

Harry Lauder (1870–1950)

Keep Buggering On.

Winston Churchill (1874–1965)

1953

There are three events, three occasions for great national rejoicing, that stand out in the British memory of 1953.

The coronation of Queen Elizabeth II on 2 June.

The ascent of Everest by Edmund Hillary of New Zealand and Sherpa Tenzing Norgay of Nepal. They were not Brits, granted, but they were on a British expedition and the news of their success arrived in London on the morning of the coronation, which was good enough for us.

The defeat of the Australians at the Oval in August and the return, after a twenty-year wait, of the Ashes.

If you say '1953?' to people of a certain age, as I have done while writing this book, they often mention two, if not all three of those events. They do not mention the terrible floods on the east coast of England, which killed over 300 people and left 30,000 homeless, nor the death of Stalin, nor the deaths of Kathleen Ferrier or Dylan Thomas. And least of all what happened on 23 June in 10 Downing Street.

That is not surprising because they were never told.

The main players

Sir Winston Churchill, the Prime Minister, 78
Lady Clementine Churchill, 68
Mr Jock Colville, the Prime Minister's secretary, 38
Lord Moran, the Prime Minister's doctor, 70
Mr Anthony Eden, the Foreign Secretary, 56
Dr Richard Cattell, an American surgeon, 55
Nurse Millie Appleyard, 28

It was pure Winston.

That was how Jock Colville put it the next morning, and he was right, it was. The Prime Minister had been on sparkling form. One moment the old boy was mischievous in his mockery, a note he particularly liked to strike, the next he was giving them one of his witty little history lessons, before lifting them all with his sober yet hopeful finale. Nor did Clementine, who was usually the first to see the way the wind was blowing, spot anything amiss. He was sailing confidently along, holding the assembled company in the palm of his hand, before reaching (in that characteristic fashion) for his glass to toast the Italians.

In their long and tumultuous life together Clementine had sat and smiled through a thousand such speeches, a thousand such humorous moments, a thousand little history lessons, not to mention a few sections of his memorably stirring oratory in which he managed to be both gloomy *and* uplifting, halting *and* spontaneous. Of course she longed for his speech to be over and the guests to be gone so that they could go upstairs to bed. Indeed, to be honest, she longed for everything to be over: all of it, the whole caboodle, the travelling circus, the Cabinet meetings and the Commons clashes, the public pomp and the private wranglings, the exhausting, protracted, all-consuming business of politics.

It was time to move over, time to move on. It was time to make way for Anthony Eden, dear Anthony, long past time in fact. But as her practised eye picked up the expressions around the table, in particular the awed faces of Signor De Gasperi and the Italian legation, she admitted to herself, for the thousandth time, albeit with rather bitter pride, that no one, not even now, could do this sort of thing better than her husband.

Confident that he could bring the ship safely into harbour without any further need to peer at his written notes, Winston took off his glasses. With all his pre-speech nerves gone, and the grumpiness that attended them, he could now bathe in his persuasive cadences and indulge in his perfectly shaped sentences.

Loyal listener though she was, Lady Churchill would have been the first to admit that – at her age and particularly at such functions – her attention was prone to wander just a little, so here is how her husband drew to his conclusion that night in 10 Downing Street, the night of 23 June 1953:

'And so, Signor De Gasperi, in drinking to your health, and to that of the whole Italian nation, I am mindful that only twice in our long and eventful history have these islands of ours ever been conquered. Only twice. But I have to tell you that we British have long memories. In 55 BC' – here he allowed himself a dramatic pause, an allowance a second too long – 'in 55 BC, as every British schoolboy knows, we were conquered for the first time. By the Romans.'

The Italians laughed and conceded the point. *Si, si, è vero.* To which the Prime Minister, enjoying the playful banter, responded with his puckish grin:

'The Romans conquered Britain, yes, but our conquerors built not only Roman cities and Roman roads and a Roman Wall, but a better way. There was law; there was order; there was peace; there was warmth; there was food, and a population free from barbarism without being sunk into sloth or luxury, beyond the luxury of a hot Roman bath, of which, throughout my long and not uneventful life, I have (as my wife will confirm) partaken twice a day.'

Signor De Gasperi bowed his head to acknowledge this praise of his nation's distant imperial past, an Italian past much prouder than the country's more recent history, while Lady Churchill smiled and nodded her confirmation of Winston's well-established bathing routine. Yes, he did love being in his tub, having a soak, and he always filled it to the brim.

'And when, five centuries later, the Roman legions finally set sail back for the warm Mediterranean, they left behind a land transfigured. The fragile civilisation of Britain, set on the fringes of the mighty Roman Empire, grew from strength to strength, until in the fullness of time, the *British* Empire, as the Roman Empire had once been, became the most powerful on earth.'

And this is where the Prime Minister took off his glasses and put down his notes.

'But while allowing ourselves briefly to peer back across the gulf of nearly two thousand years we must, in these feverish and precarious days of 1953, lose no opportunity to ease the difficulties which at present divide and bedevil the world. For in this Atomic Age we have the power to blow ourselves to pieces in a matter of months, if not minutes. In modern Europe, perilously riven as it is, *all* countries must cast off fear and make the proper use of their gifts to benefit mankind. That will be the spirit in which I shall sail next week to Bermuda ... sail in HMS *Vanguard* ... next week ... to Ber-mu-da to meet with President Eisenhower, so strong is my desire to achieve a summit and a generation of peace with Soviet Russia ... in these post-Stalin days.

'And in that spirit, in the spirit of hope, I ask everyone to rise ... I give you Signor De Gap ... Signor De Gas ... And the nation of ... '

Smiling purposefully as he slipped round behind the long dining room table, his face an unflappable mask, Jock Colville was the first to be at the Prime Minister's side. As the table rose and raised their glasses, he had seen Sir Winston land heavily back on his seat. As the table went up the Prime Minister went down. Colville had also seen Churchill's head very slowly slump to the right.

He leant over his shoulder, whispering:

'Prime Minister? Are you all right?'

'What?'

'A glass of water perhaps?'

'Am – I?'

'It's very hot in here, isn't it? Stifling. Shall we open a window?'

Churchill's fingers waved in the general direction of his notes.

'How – did – it . . . ?'

'The speech went very well. Some lovely touches. They absolutely lapped it up.'

The Prime Minister stared at him as if at a fool.

'Lapped?'

Clementine was now at his other side. She gripped his arm, trying to adjust his position on the seat, trying to re-settle him as if all was normal.

'Winston? What is it?'

'How – how – did . . . ?'

'Shall I get him some water? There's none in his glass.'

'No, get Charles here. Immediately!'

'Of course.'

'Don't say anything, Jock. Not a word to anyone.'

'Of course not.'

'And do your best to get Signor De Gasperi and the guests to leave. As soon as possible, and above all we don't want any murmuring.'

'There won't be.'

'Minimum fuss.'

'Absolutely.'

'Nothing for the papers.'

'Of course not.'

'And ring Charles.'

The Prime Minister, pale and heavy, slowly tilted his face towards his wife, essaying a smile.

'Cat?'

'Yes, Winston?'

'How – did – it . . . ?'

'Don't fret about all that. It was perfect. You must lie down, that's all. You're over-tired. You can't say I didn't warn you, but you won't listen, will you?'

'Lie? Where?'

'And one thing is certain. This puts an end to that ridiculous Bermuda business. I've never heard such nonsense.'

Jock Colville was now out of the room, doing as he was bidden, but Charles Moran, just when you most needed him, was not answering his telephone.

*

Charles McMoran Wilson – Lord Moran since 1943 – bustled in, Gladstone bag in hand, only to find his way blocked by the Prime Minister's secretary.

'Ah, Charles, you're here.'

There are, as they say, ways and ways of saying things, and the way young Jock Colville said the four words 'Ah, Charles, you're here' grated with the old doctor. It grated quite a lot. Indeed, he would go further: it made him dyspeptic. Coming from Northern Irish stock, and with a Yorkshire grammar school education, Moran did not take kindly at the best of times – and these were not the best of times – to the languid voice of this smooth young diplomat, his public school tones textured with practised implication, the implication being that with just a little more effort and despatch the President of the Royal College of Physicians could have been at the Prime

Minister's bedside some hours ear
argue that the smooth young diploma
message and not a million miles off saying
old stick, 'And where the hell have you been

'I was out to dinner last night. In Sussex.'

'Ah, that would explain it.'

'In Horsham.'

'In *Hor*sham? *Were* you?'

The affected disbelief with which Colville pronounced *Horsham,* suggesting it could as well have been Hackney or Honolulu, was more than enough for the dyspeptic Moran, who barked back,

'Is he in bed?'

Indeed he was, but Colville allowed himself a second or two before saying,

'Mrs Churchill would like you to call on her when you've finished, if you wouldn't mind.'

'Mind? Why should I?'

Not batting an eyelid, Colville half raised a conciliatory palm.

'It's just that she feels very strongly that—'

'Of course I'll see her. I always do.'

Colville nodded and his highly polished shoes took a few paces to one side, as if conceding that Moran had now, after due and careful consideration of all the circumstances, been granted access to the inner circle.

'Thank you. Do go through.'

But Lord Moran did not go through. He put his medical bag huffily down on a chair. He would go through when he was bloody ready to go through and not one minute before, and certainly not at the beck and call of Jock Colville.

The telephone had rung at his home in Hassocks just before midnight. Dorothy was beside him in bed – they were both reading – but even before he had put down his cocoa and picked up his spectacles Lord Moran felt a prickle of apprehension. The telephone, nearly always, was trouble. Winston trouble. Only Number 10 would contact him at so late an hour. Not that the girl on the exchange would add much to the basic facts, oh no, she was far too well trained for that, she simply repeated the request that Lord Moran attend the Prime Minister at nine in the morning.

There was a dog howling somewhere and Moran hardly slept a wink. He saw that June dawn breaking at 3.45 and he banged his head on the pillow and shut his eyes tight for the fiftieth time. But it was no good, he was up at 4.55 and pacing around the kitchen in rather a stew. And even after the earliest of starts on the road it had been a difficult drive up to town, part of which was spent recalling the numerous medical crises in his patient's life, or 'hurdles' as Winston preferred to call them.

And hurdles there had been aplenty. Each episode was stamped on Moran's mind; each struggle to keep the old carcass going had been stressful. There had been the Prime Minister's pneumonia in 1943, starting with a heavy cold in Algiers and exacerbated by a long flight in a freezing bomber; there had been the slight stroke he suffered in Monte Carlo in 1949, and the heart scare in

New York; then there were the sudden depressions, the black dogs; and the diverticulitis, not to mention the numerous lesser ailments, the palpitations, the conjunctivitis and the throat problems, the wobbly legs, the giddy spells, the promises to give up smoking, the tingly fingers, the swelling in his groin, the rupture and all that humiliating worry over whether or not to wear a truss.

Twelve years and still counting Lord Moran had spent looking after Winston. Twelve years in war and in peace, twelve years in office and out of office, day in day out, twelve years trying to keep the cigar alight, with an increasing number of pills (the reds and the whites) and capsules and sachets, and even then he could never tell whether or not the old boy was played out. Quite simply, he was not like other men. One day you thought it was all up with him and he looked about to keel over, only to find him later that night, brandy in hand, holding court in Chartwell, when no power on earth could stop him singing 'A Wandering Minstrel, I', or 'Lily of Laguna'.

And here the old doctor, who had spent three long years of his youth in the trenches, was being patronised by Master Jock Colville, who only found himself in Number 10 and doing what he was doing because he was related to everyone from the Queen down and connected to everyone else; and, of course, he had gone to the same school as WSC, to wit, Harrow.

Looking at Colville now, and trying to overcome his distaste, Moran could not ever imagine the Prime Minister's secretary slapping a golf ball down the fairway or making a try-saving tackle at rugger. It was clear from the briefest assessment that Colville would never have made any school team picked by Moran, let alone been considered for one of his St Mary's Hospital sides. Touch judge at best.

'Were you actually watching?' Moran asked the touch judge.

'Watching?'

'When it happened.'

'No, we were all on our feet, toasting the Italians. Something of a new experience.'

The doctor looked blank. Had he missed some private joke? If so, it wouldn't be for the first time. Moran found he rarely 'got' jokes, so he did not join in group laughter. Nor did he sing dirty rugger songs, and unsurprisingly (given all this) he had never been considered a good mixer.

'What was new about the experience?'

'Toasting the Italians.'

'Not with you, I'm afraid.'

'Our brave allies in the war? Never mind. The Italian delegation were our guests at dinner.'

'So they all saw it?'

'No, very few saw anything.'

'I hope you're right.'

With all the plotting and hounding going on, the last thing the Prime Minister needed was another health rumour mill, another chance for one of Anthony Eden's people to talk about passing on the baton, or to take you to one side to whisper the word *ga-ga.* In Westminster rumours and insurrections sprang up overnight, like mushrooms.

'But,' Colville said, 'I suspect those who did see something thought the Prime Minister may have drunk too much.'

'Drunk too much?'

'Might have been a bit the worse for wear.'

Drunk too much? *The worse for wear?* Moran's hands ticked with annoyance. Why did Winston always risk going too far? How many times had he told him about the dangers of over-indulgence, of over-eating, of over-drinking, not to mention too many cigars, and above all how many times had he told him never to mix the pills (red or white) with the champagne?

As for his own habits, Moran never drank more than a single dry sherry before dinner. Just the one and then his hand went firmly over his glass. If Moran was a connoisseur of any drink it was good clear water, which was why Winston liked to mock what he called his doctor's monkish streak.

'But he hadn't drunk too much?'

'No, not a bit of it. He was on top form, made a brilliant little speech. Pure Winston, it really was. Winston neat and undiluted.'

Moran was not comfortable with all this Winston-this-Winston-that over-familiarity. The simple words 'Prime Minister' would do. A few old-fashioned manners from the young man wouldn't go amiss. For all his family background, Colville would do well to stick to the facts and remember that he was only the Prime Minister's secretary.

'So it was very sudden?' Moran asked.

'As far as one could see from the other side of the table.'

'What about the waiters?'

'I'm sorry?'

'You heard. I said what about the waiters.'

Colville shook his head.

'There won't be any murmurings. Don't you worry, I've seen to that.'

'And he walked up to his bedroom?'

'We got him into the lift. With a little help.'

Though it went against the grain, Moran did wonder if this might be the right moment to ask Colville the indiscreet and disquieting question, but before he could even fully consider the risks involved in such a course he found that he had asked it out loud:

'Did the Prime Minister know, before this happened to him, how bad Eden is? Had anyone briefed him on how things are in Boston?'

To this unexpected delivery Colville played, after the slightest of smiles, the straightest of bats:

'I am not aware how much the Prime Minister knew, or knows, about Mr Eden's condition.'

With his hackles raised, Moran picked up his bag and strode straight past him.

*

In certain moods, according to Winston, particularly when she had something pressing on her mind, Lady Churchill was prone to lie in wait before landing on him like a jaguar from a tree. Well, she now landed like a jaguar from a tree on her husband's personal physician, and well before he could knock on the Prime Minister's bedroom door.

'Oh, thank God you're here.'

'Good morning, Clementine.'

She barred his way. Fireworks ahead.

'I saw this coming, Charles. I said this would happen, I *said* it.'

'Did you?'

'I have been saying it for months. I saw the signs.'

'Yes, well, we all warned him.'

Lady Churchill seemed taller and stronger with every word she emphatically spoke:

'But *did* you, Charles? Did you?'

'Yes, I did. Countless times.'

Her voice continued to rise. Her eyes were blazing.

'But he didn't listen, did he?'

'No, he often doesn't listen. As you would know better than any of us.'

'So what help are you? What *good* are you?'

'Would you like me to examine him?'

'That's exactly what we're all waiting for.'

'Because before I can say anything of value to you this morning I should give him a thorough examination. There are no miracle cures for a man of his age. So, if you'll excuse me . . .'

As Lord Moran went along the carpet to the bedroom door Lady Churchill glared at his back. And then she saw red.

'And what on earth *kept* you?'

*

The room was hot and airless, almost a fug. For an irritable moment, as he opened the window a couple of notches and looked out at Horse Guards Parade, Moran suspected that Winston had been secretly smoking. He was quite capable of it, even when stricken. But there were no giveaway signs that he had: no cigar box in sight, no anti-slobber device in the ashtray, and no lingering blue in the narrow shafts of sunlight.

Moran moved a step forward. Then he stood stock still, as if on parade and at attention. He watched and listened. Winston had nothing on but one of his favourite silk vests. Inappropriate parallel or not, to Moran his patient looked at that moment a little like a pugnaciously dozing Mr Samuel Pickwick. His eyes were closed and his breathing was quite heavy.

'So, what's all this, eh?'

Churchill did not stir. Moran took two more steps and sat at the head of the bed:

'What have you been up to this time?'

There was no response. Then, without opening his eyes, Churchill began to speak, *pill, pill, turn the, turn the,* then he flapped a hand and seemed to give up, only to start all over again.

'Turn the … pillow over, would you?'

'The pillow, of course.'

'I've got a tingling.'

'Have you?'

'In my … cheeks.'

His voice came and went like a faultily tuned wireless. Moran gently lifted him up and held his shoulders.

'It's Charles here.'

'Yes, it is Charles, isn't it?'

'Just give me a moment, would you?'

Moran turned Churchill's pillow and slowly eased him back down. The Prime Minister nodded.

'Cooler. Yes. That's cool-er.'

'Dear oh dear. It's one thing after another, isn't it?'

'After what?'

'After another. One thing after another, I said. We could have done without this. So let's have a look at you, shall we?'

'What? What is it?'

The Prime Minister half opened his eyes and said,

'You haven't taken my pulse.'

Moran shook his head and sat back.

'You never change, do you?'

'But I have. There is a … change. That's the point. I can feel it.'

'What can you feel?'

'I'm all at sea. Listen with your … stetho, your stethoscope, if you've remembered to bring it. Have you brought it? Always … bring it.'

'Thank you for the advice.'

The Prime Minister fumbled for Moran's arm and shakily pressed it.

'Tell me straight, Charles.'

'Oh, I will, don't worry.'

'Only short words. Short words and ... vulgar fractions.'

'You and your short words and your vulgar fractions.'

'And tell me something else. I've been thinking.'

He again waved his hand in a slow circle.

'Yes?' Moran said.

'Been thinking a lot.'

'Yes?'

'Where the hell is Guatemala?'

'Search me. Not my subject.'

'I've been trying to work it out.'

'I think I'd leave that for another day, if I were you.'

'Cam-bo-di-a? Any idea?'

'At the moment I am trying to concentrate but all you are doing is delaying me with your ridiculous questions. Will you please be quiet. And squeeze my left hand. Squeeze. Harder, if you can. Is that your hardest? Thank you.'

Churchill released his grip and shrugged. A flicker of his naughty-boy-told-off expression passed over his face, but it did not last long.

'Am I more dead than alive? On balance?'

'Not a helpful discussion.'

'You haven't taken my pulse yet. And my foot is twitching.'

'I can see why Lady Churchill is exasperated. I'll check all that in a moment.'

'Been at you, has she? Chief of Staff?'

'Not a bit of it.'

'Oh yes she has.'

'Not at all.'

'Bit of a . . . showdown, eh? Bit of a hulla-balloo?'

'Right, I need to check your blood pressure and, you'll be glad to hear, your pulse. And, if I may, I will listen to your chest. Winston, I do need to do these checks.'

The Prime Minister closed his eyes and seemed to be lumpish.

'Oh, all right.'

'Thank you.'

'Charles?'

'What now?'

'I can feel there's a . . . '

'A what?'

Churchill slowly raised and slowly lowered his hand to rest on the bedclothes.

'A veil.'

For a moment or so the Prime Minister was obediently quiet, his mouth set, his soft, feminine hands lying still. Moran thought he might have slipped away (as he often did at the best of times) into a brief sleep, until he heard,

'So I am near my end?'

Moran ignored this.

'I am glad now that it is the end.'

Moran ignored this as well.

'Are you at all concerned, Charles, as my doctor, that I am nearing my end?'

'I am trying to examine you. That is my concern at the moment.'

'So. So, my friend, I am in your clutches once more.'

'I wouldn't put it that way. But I would like you to see Brain.'

'Brain?'

'Sir Russell Brain, he's been here before.'

'Brain?'

'He's a good man. A sound judge. He took over from me as President.'

'Ah, that Brain. Whatshisname Brain. Sir Whatsit Brain. About my brain? Ginger me up, you mean? You're right. There's no vim, is there?'

He pointed towards his chest. 'And my heart is doing something funny. Did you notice that?'

Vim or no vim, funny heart or no funny heart, the Prime Minister had a pale greyish look about his gills. And his eyes weren't right. Time for the ophthalmoscope.

*

On many a day, even a turbulent one, Clementine found she could sit quietly with Jock Colville. He was an amiable young man who knew how to behave. She liked him. He could almost have been a son of hers, and a much easier one he would have been than dear Randolph. She took comfort from his calming presence, and his quiet attentiveness worked particularly well if she was feeling a little tender. But today she was beyond tender and beyond calming.

'It's all bad. I can feel it in my bones.'

'Oh, I'm sure he'll be—'

'No, no, no, it's clear, he's killed himself with overwork.'

'Let's see what Charles has to say, shall we?'

'What do you think is going on in there?'

'He'll be out soon, and all will be revealed.'

'Has Anthony been told?'

'Yes, I spoke to Shuckburgh, and a message has been sent to Boston. To Clarissa in fact. They know the position.'

'Poor Clarissa. She's too young, far too young for all this. Just a young gel and barely married.'

Eden's second wife, Clarissa – and another Churchill, in fact she was Winston and Clementine's niece – was over twenty years younger than her husband. She had accompanied Eden to Boston for the surgery.

'More coffee?'

'Just a splash.'

'How's that?'

'Plenty, Jock, thank you. Do you know Shuckburgh well?'

'Evelyn? Fairly. I've always found him very helpful. One of those terribly clever Wykehamists you find all over the place. And rather highly strung.'

'No more than Anthony, I trust!'

'On the same lines.'

'But loyal?'

'Oh, I'm sure.'

Loyal private secretary though he was, Evelyn Shuckburgh, like many who had been to Winchester College, was not above a waspish word. Over an unguarded late night glass with Colville, he had once described Eden as a sea anemone, covered all over with sensitive tentacles, quivering as they strove to pick up every tiny current of opinion about himself and his popularity and his policies. And if a sea anemone could be said to fly off the handle, there was that as well.

If he was prepared to develop that analogy about Eden, it didn't take much imagination to work out the sort of things the loyal Shuckburgh would come up with about Winston, the old man who was still standing in Eden's way: the old boy's going senile, living in the past, coddled in a closed court, thinks he's the only one who can unfreeze the Cold War, only he doesn't even read his papers, only wants to be told what he wants to hear, expects his every whim to be indulged and can't even finish his sentences, etc.

For his part, Colville almost found himself saying to Shuckburgh that if Eden pressed Winston too hard it would be seen as further proof that he wasn't mature enough to take charge, wasn't ready to move into Number 10. Winston, who dreaded solitude and the very thought of oblivion, would be far more likely to go if he was treated kindly and felt he wasn't being pushed.

'And now,' Clementine said, 'we've no Winston and Anthony's at death's door. What a pickle we're in.'

'We'll manage the tide,' Colville said. 'We'll get through this. We've all been through worse.'

'Have we?'

'And I'm told Cattell is a genius on gall bladders.'

'Cattell?'

'The American surgeon. Apparently we English suffer more from ulcers, from our lack of fats and so forth, while the Americans do rather tuck into their grub and are as a consequence constantly having gall bladder issues, so the surgeon's had much more opportunity to use his knife.'

'Anthony looked a terrible colour when he left, didn't he?'

'Did he?'

'I thought so. Like a skeleton.'

'He'd lost a lot of weight.'

'If it's not aspirin with Anthony it's morphine. Have you ever seen his medicine box? The tin one he carries with him. You've never noticed? He's always had something wrong with his insides.'

'He's in pain a great deal, Shuckburgh says. Dogged by it.'

'Always difficult, though, isn't it, to judge the level of pain with thoroughbreds. He loves flowers, you know, Anthony does.'

'Does he?'

'Loves them. I always think that's rather a good thing in a man.'

'Interesting.'

'How long does it take to recover from that sort of operation? The one this American chap is always doing?'

'Best ask Charles.'

'Oh, I will, don't you worry. And I'll be asking him something else as well.'

The atmosphere had changed. They looked at each other in the stillness. What was going on now?

'Jock?'

'Yes?'

'Do you think he's keeping a diary?'

'Who?'

'Charles, of course.'

'Oh, surely not. No, he wouldn't.'

'He wouldn't?'

'Charles knows the form.'

'Does he?'

'Well, no, he doesn't, generally speaking.'

'And he's never really . . . belonged.'

'But on this issue . . . on this issue I'm sure he wouldn't go that far.'

'I'm not keeping you, Jock, am I? Keeping you from your work?'

'Not at all.'

'It's so kind of you to sit with me.'

'Not a bit.'

'Because . . . the thing is . . . '

She reached across and put her hand on his.

'Jock, dear.'

'Yes.'

'I wonder if I could ask you something. It's rather a great favour, I'm afraid. But I do need your help.'

'Ask away, please.'

'It's something very special. And I don't think I can manage this one on my own.'

'You know I'd do anything for you. What is it?'

'Persuade Winston to stand down. Persuade him to retire. Now. Promise me you will.'

*

Moran put down the ophthalmoscope and straightened up, sensing he might as well fire the first shot over the Prime Minister's bows.

'Well, your circulation does seem a little sluggish. Too early to be sure, of course, but I think it may have been a spasm in a small artery.'

'Spasm?'

'It looks to me more or less in the same family as the Monte Carlo incident.'

'Monte Carlo?'

The word 'spasm' did the job. The Prime Minister's flippant boyishness gave way to anxious eyes. And, as was his habit, he slipped straight into his old game of returning a phrase, which sometimes suggested that he was playing for time or, less often, that he was genuinely confused. Moran had seen both and been foxed by both, so he tried to keep his own tone even.

'You remember, a few years back, in 1949, when you found it difficult to squeeze the paint out of the tubes?

You were on a painting trip in France. You were staying with Max in his villa there. Max? Max Beaverbrook? Anyway you were, and I flew down to Nice to see you. It was a very small clot.'

'A Monte Carlo clot, then?'

'Let's hope so.'

'And this clot is a . . . potential aggressor? A little *Nar-zee*?'

'It is. So I'd like you to behave yourself for a day or two while I make some arrangements. You sit tight until we see how things are. And do nothing. *Nothing*. The brain is a very complicated thing. Billions of connections.'

'Billions?'

'At least.'

Churchill started to grin. A bit lopsidedly.

'That's very precise of you. Billions.'

'No one really knows how many.'

'But quite a few of mine will still be working?'

'Oh, more than enough.'

'And if you pep me up with a few of your red pills?'

'What on earth are you talking about?'

'Call . . . call . . . get what's-his-name.'

'Who?'

'Get Jock-wotcher-cock in here. I took grave exception to his moustache, you know.'

'Whose moustache?'

'Wotcher-cock's! Jock's! You must remember, when he joined the RAF. As soon as I saw it, it had to go. And there's that privy councillor, isn't there, whatsisname, he's got a moustache.'

'There are a few of those around.'

'Well, they've got to go. All of them.'

'Anthony has a moustache.'

'Good point. Anyway, get him in here.'

'Anthony?'

'*Will you please listen!* I said Jock.'

Moran found himself getting angry as well.

'Jock? Jock Colville? Now?'

'Yes. I have a Cabinet meeting at eleven.'

'Win-*ston*!'

The Prime Minister jutted out his jaw.

'Then I have to go to the House. It's Wednesday, isn't it?'

'The House of Commons? The House of Commons today! Don't be ridiculous.'

'Brings the best out in me. And I've still got millions of brain cells. If not billions. You just said so. Anyway, quite enough brain cells to give the socialists a good kicking. An-eur-rin Bev-*an*! I'll start with him. And you said I needed gingering up. So send for Jock's-his-name. He'll tell me how many questions there are for ... the Prime Minister. That's me. And the Foreign Secretary. That's me too. With no Anthony.'

'Winston, I will be frank with you.'

Churchill sat up on one elbow, rocked a bit, and allowed his right foot to appear and then dangle over the side of the bed.

'Oh, don't start all that, Charles. You're always being frank. Frank this frank that. Your parents should have called you Frank. I've no patience with people who are always raising difficulties.'

'I strongly advise against the Cabinet meeting. And if you go to the House—'

He very slowly swung his whole right leg over the side of the bed.

'I *am* going—'

'If you go to the House I cannot guarantee that you will use the right word. That is, if you manage to remain standing up in the first place. Things could be a lot worse with you in a few hours' time. You might rise to your feet and find that no words come to you at all. I'm afraid I do have to make that clear to you. *No words!*'

The Prime Minister's mouth sagged open.

'No words?'

'Which coming from you would be quite something. Especially in the House.'

'You are saying—'

'That is what I am saying! Have I not made myself clear? Right, I want to check your eyes again. You weren't very helpful a moment ago. Could you open them a little wider? Look straight into my eyes. That's it. Won't be long.'

After the check on the retinas was done, the Prime Minister leant back on his pillows. His voice, when it came, was petulant.

'Oh, all right. I'll take the Cabinet downstairs, but I won't go . . . to the House. On doctor's orders.'

Moran responded in a gentler tone.

'No, not today at any rate. One day at a time, eh?'

'Bow to my fate, is that it? Give in?'

'No one is suggesting that. Least of all me. And least of all to you.'

'Bloody business, isn't it? Life.'

'Doesn't have to be. And better this than the trenches. Better this than the Blitz.'

'So, if this goes on, who will, then?'

'What?'

'Take over.'

'Not my affair, I'm glad to say.'

Moran closed his bag and moved towards the door.

'Mind you, Charles, Anthony will be relieved.'

'Anthony? Will he?'

'Don't be bloody obtuse.'

'I don't follow.'

'He must have thought I'd go on for ever.'

'As a matter of fact, Anthony might not go on all that long himself.'

But the Prime Minister was not listening. He was now hoarsely self-dramatising.

'And ever. A-men.'

'Winston, what on earth am I going to do with you?'

'Come back, dear Charles, won't you? I'll see you after the Cabinet. When one is faced with a foe, such as the . . . circulatory clot, one turns to one's faithful friends.'

'Clementine would like to see me.'

'Oh, better be off then. Better run along.'

With his hand on the door knob and straightening the edge of the carpet with his foot, Moran said,

'As for you, please try to do what you are told. This is serious.'

'Charles, dear boy, just . . . one thing?'

'Yes?'

'Where are the goldfish?'

*

The scrub nurse was slow, just the once, slow to sponge away Mr Eden's blood. She was only a split second late in anticipating what he wanted, but that was enough time for Dr Cattell to do it himself before whispering (so quietly that no one else on the team heard), 'I expect you to be there first.' From the gentlest of gentlemen who would permit no harsh words to be said of anyone, this was criticism enough, the most astringent he would ever be, and she felt the stab. Letting Dr Cattell down in the operating room was the worst of feelings.

As far as was possible, Richard Bartley Channing Cattell, to give the surgeon his full collection of Christian names, liked bloodless surgery. Indeed, he prided himself on bloodless surgery. Even more, however, he asked for total concentration from his close-knit team. They all had to concentrate all the time. They had to be primed. There were to be no jokes, no comments and no inappropriate asides because in the operating room it was the case and nothing but the case.

Straight talk not small talk. 'Work hard or get out' had been the class motto in his Peabody High School days in Ohio and he took that motto every day into the Lahey Clinic in Boston.

Six foot three in his socks, with painful hammer toes on both feet, the long-limbed and long-fingered Dr Cattell did sometimes hum when things were going particularly well, but on that June morning in 1953 there was no humming. From the moment, scrubbed, capped, gowned and gloved, Dr Cattell had opened up the British Foreign Secretary he could see the full extent of the problem.

One abdominal incision was all it took.

His photographic memory stored all he saw. Eden's face might be suntanned, albeit with a yellowish tinge, but more to the point, his insides were a mess, with scarring, adhesions and disruption of the normal architecture. If the surgeon needed immediate confirmation of his findings, the grim faces of his medical colleagues reinforced his fears.

And Cattell knew the score: get this one right and the famous Englishman's health would be restored, but no one would be given any credit because Cattell was expected to get it right. Get it wrong, and there would be nothing but English criticism of the American. That's what the English were like.

He turned to his scrub nurse.

'Right. Are we ready? Here we go.'

*

Having left the stricken Prime Minister, Moran stood for a moment outside Lady Churchill's drawing room door, collecting himself, if not steeling himself. He knew Clementine was in there and he knew exactly where she would be sitting. Come on, man, it's not life and death, get it over and done with. If there's a scene there's a scene.

He knocked and entered. Her room was feminine, all small pieces, mahogany this and walnut that, not that he was interested.

'May I sit down?'

'Of course, Charles.'

Lady Churchill was at her small writing table in the corner of the room. She took off her reading spectacles and fiddled with them in her lap as she spoke.

'I can only ask your forgiveness, Charles, for earlier. I didn't mean to put you on the spot.'

'Don't give it another thought.'

'But you were in there ages.'

'Thirty-five, forty minutes. It wasn't something to rush.'

'How serious is it?'

'Difficult to say. That's why I'm asking Brain to see him.'

'Please don't beat about the bush.'

'I think we can agree that I do not usually beat about the bush.'

'Forgive me, again.'

'Again, don't give it another thought.'

She stood up, flaring at his riposte.

'There was no need to be smart with me. This is my husband's life.'

Moran stood up and met her glare.

'I know that very well, Clementine, so why don't you

listen, unless you are a doctor as well? There may be restricted blood flow or a clot. A clot lodges in the artery and something stops working. Or half stops. Or less. Sometimes a small haemorrhage can result in extensive paralysis.'

'Which he hasn't got. And he's talking.'

Moran did not respond.

'He *is* still talking, isn't he?'

'Yes, at times he was quite perky. There's no such thing as the law of an average stroke and if there were, Winston would be first in the queue to flout it. The concept of a law of averages just provokes him. Who knows what tomorrow will bring? He may be better or he may be unable to move or to formulate speech or to see one side of a visual field. In effect his brain may be injured, and we're waiting to see the extent of the injury.'

'But should we be waiting?'

'I am not sure you are listening. If you'll permit me to—'

'Shouldn't you be *doing* something?'

'It's never easy to predict. I can't be sure there's no irreversible or permanent damage. If it's transient it can be as little as twenty-four to thirty-six hours. Anyway, don't let's cross bridges. I'll tell you the answers if and when I know the answers.'

'Doing two jobs at his age! The two biggest jobs in the country at nearly eighty! Anthony falls very ill so what does Winston do, he takes over foreign affairs as well because he can't delegate and because no one else is of course up to it and you stand by and watch. It's madness. Utter madness!'

'Clementine, I am not a politician, I am a doc—'

'And one thing is certain. This ridiculous Bermuda Conference, this summit with Eisenhower, is out of the question. Out of the question! He said he was only hanging on until the coronation, so what did we do, we hung on for the coronation. And now where is he? I'll tell you where, he is hanging on by a thread. Well, at long last he is going to listen to me, not to you and his cronies. Charles, do you hear me?'

'I heard the word *cronies* very clearly.'

'Yes, Beaverbrook, Bracken, all of you. I'm sorry but you are, and you're all gambling with his life. He is not the man he was.'

'Don't talk to me about gambling. Winston is the gambler, Clementine, not me. He's never been one to count the coins in his pocket.'

'How dare you speak to me like that!'

'He says he wants to take the Cabinet.'

'No.'

'Yes, later this morning.'

'No, no, *no*!'

'I told him that.'

'Tell him again.'

'I have done. Very firmly. You tackle him.'

'No, *you* tackle him! You're the great rugger player!'

'But I can't strap him to his bed, can I, and he can speak and he can sit in a chair. You could always lock the door on him, I suppose.'

Clementine walked around the room. She turned slowly, and when she spoke it was with cold deliberation.

'There's something else I've been meaning to ask you.'

'Yes?'

'You're not writing it all down, are you? About what Winston goes through? About all this?'

Moran just managed to keep control of his voice.

'A doctor has to take notes.'

'*Notes?*'

'Which I can then consult. Winston is not one of the world's listeners at the best of times, and I find he is marginally more likely to pay attention if I can refer to earlier instances.'

'He didn't listen to you after his heart attack.'

'No. He didn't after the stroke in Monte Carlo either.'

'No.'

'And he didn't after his pneumonia. He didn't in Cairo. Nor after the business in Washington. I think we can agree he doesn't listen much at all. But I do keep essential medical notes. Medical notes, not gossip.'

'As long as we are clear about the difference.'

'He tells me my job is to see off the bugs. Or, as now, an even greater enemy. My job is to keep him going.'

'Yes, yes, go ahead! Go ahead and patch him up! Go and tell him he's the only one who can save the world. Tell him he was the Father of the Victory and now he's going to be the Father of the Peace. Keep him going with your pills until he drops. I'll tell you what you are doing, Charles, and it is as clear as day. You are aiding and abetting in a disaster.'

'That's not true.'

'And you're frightened of him.'

'Not a bit.'

'Yes you are.'

'Not one little bit. I'm not frightened of anyone.'

'It's the same with Anthony. He's very strong outside the door, he goes in, and trots back out like a lamb.'

'Anthony won't be doing much trotting for a while.'

'What is the latest?'

'I imagine Jock will have told you. If I find out any more this afternoon I'll let you know.'

'Poor Anthony.'

He turned at the door.

'Clementine.'

'Yes?'

'One more thing about Winston.'

'Yes?'

'He was looking for the goldfish tank.'

Clementine put her head in her hands.

'Chartwell! My God. He thought he was in Chartwell?'

'Yes, which is where he should be in my view. And as soon as possible.'

'I quite agree. You couldn't be more right. But who would be there to nurse him? I would need all the help I could muster.'

'I'll see to that straight away. I know who to ask.'

*

Two months earlier, in St Bartholomew's Hospital in London, with Mr Eden on the operating table, the knife in an English surgeon's hand had unfortunately slipped. Or that was how the prickly Charles Moran, sitting in 10 Downing Street, had put it to Dr Cattell.

Humanum est errare, we all make mistakes, it can happen to any of us at any time, Moran implied, his eyes coercive, his eyes challenging Dr Cattell to disagree. It can happen even to one of the finest surgeons, and no surgeon on earth (according to Lord Moran) was better than a top English surgeon. Except that the knife had never slipped in Dr Cattell's hand, not once in over eleven hundred major operations, nor in the hand of any of his team in the Lahey Clinic.

That inadvertent slip – that moment of English incompetence in April 1953 – had cut apart Eden's common bile duct, releasing dangerous body poisons into his system. You could argue that his constitution had never been of the strongest in the first place, but however you viewed his natural strength, the Foreign Secretary's health had now collapsed. Not only were his political ambitions and career in jeopardy, his very life was in the balance. On one thing, however, all his doctors eventually agreed: he would never recover unless he underwent a third operation.

On a lecture tour to London in that same month, April 1953, Cattell heard for the first time of the Foreign Secretary's worsening plight and spoke to Sir Horace Evans, Eden's doctor. Within two days Cattell was whisked off to 10 Downing Street to meet the Prime Minister, in whose presence he felt a little like a schoolboy hauled up in front of his headmaster.

The legendary leader was much shorter than Cattell expected, though just as round. As for the most imitated lisp in the Western world, that was soon in evidence, as was the puckish grin, the boyish twinkle to which Americans naturally warmed. Churchill had small, soft, almost ladylike hands, misleading hands, though his grip was firm enough.

'It's extremely good of you to come and see me. To discuss what we are going to do with our dear friend.'

'It will be an honour to help you, sir, in any way. If I can.'

'And may I introduce you to Lord Moran, my doctor, the man charged with keeping this old carcass alive and kicking, as well as being a most distinguished President of the Royal College of Physicians.'

'Lord Moran. How do you do, sir.'

'How do you do, Dr Cattell.'

With the slight stoop of the very tall, Cattell looked down on the sharp-nosed Moran, whose eyes glared back up at the American surgeon with the lantern jaw.

'Do sit down, gentlemen.'

While the two doctors sat facing each other across the carpet, the Prime Minister remained standing, resting one hand on the edge of his desk, with the thumb of his other hand in his waistcoat pocket. Right, Cattell thought, that's the Old World charm done, now for the business, now for Action This Day.

But the American misjudged that. There was more English flattery, or was it calculated benevolence, to come.

'Lord Moran tells me that you are held in the highest possible repute in your field in America, that you have more experience of gall bladder operations, heaven help us, than any man on God's earth, and you are admired universally in the medical world.'

Cattell nodded his gratitude to the Prime Minister. For fifteen years he had also been an expert on the thyroid, the rectum, the pancreas and the colon before becoming famous for his work on the gall bladder, but he merely relied on his stock response:

'I work with a great team, sir.'

'And, like many of your countrymen, I see you are modest to a fault. Not to mention having a more than passing resemblance to Burt Lancaster.'

'I will inform my wife, sir. She will be surprised and pleased to hear it.'

'So. So, you have been to Chequers to see Mr Eden?'

'Yes, I was driven to Buckinghamshire yesterday.'

'And you enjoyed your time at Chequers?'

'It's a fine country residence. Most handsome.'

'I have placed it at Anthony's disposal for as long as is necessary, so that he can rest and recuperate. Rest and recuperate. And what better use could there be for Chequers, because I need Mr Eden back on his feet and firing on all cylinders. We all need him. He is a vital man, a vital cog, in these difficult times, in these . . . post-Stalin days.'

Ah, Cattell noted, the lisp. Everyone knew and imitated these Churchillian pronunciations. Stalin, the Nazis and the Gestapo were now *Shtal-een*, the *Nar-zees* and the *Gesh-taapo.*

The Prime Minister continued:

'Mr Eden knows the East, he speaks their languages, and he knows the West, of course, no man better. And we have been through so much together, he and I, including the darkest hours of the darkest days in 1940 when, as you may recall, Dr Cattell, we faced the enemy alone.'

'Indeed, sir.'

Lord Moran was nodding. And where were you lot?

'And in the fullness of time, who knows when, it is anticipated that Mr Eden will succeed me as Prime Minister.'

'If that is the situation, sir, this case is even more urgent.'

'But that's more than enough from me. How did *you* find Anthony?'

Moran edged forward a little in his seat. After a brief pause to order his thoughts the American spoke with quiet, equal emphasis, weighing each word with surgical care.

'I gave him a thorough examination in his bedroom. We were together one hour. He is very thin. He is very weak, as is consistent with his condition. He has endured two duodenal ulcers, both debilitating, he has had gall bladder problems, with two poor procedures, multiple infections and inappropriate treatments. There is little doubt in my mind that he can expect to experience further high fevers and further episodes of jaundice.'

Inappropriate! The President of the Royal College of Physicians stirred and stiffened at this slight on the reputation of his profession, a blow on the nose of British surgery:

'*In*-appropriate treatments?'

'Charles!'

'Is that what you just said?'

'Charles, Dr Cattell was answering my question with commendable frankness. And I expected no less.'

Moran leant right back in his chair, his jaw firmly set, his mouth clenched tight.

'Do go on, Dr Cattell.'

'It is my clinical opinion, sir, that a third operation is required. As a matter of the gravest urgency. It is difficult to be precise without doing an exploratory internal procedure myself but it seems clear that the first procedure, which should have been routine, was mishandled, the second little better than a salvage operation. After my examination, when Mr Eden insisted on getting dressed and coming downstairs, I sat with him in the garden at Chequers for a while, enjoying the sunshine. We talked of his times in Washington and New York. He is a most charming man.'

'Yes, Anthony does love the sunshine. He is affectionately known as the man with a tan.'

'And while there, I made a sketch to show him what I believe is required.'

'A sketch?' The notion seemed to amuse the Prime Minister.

'I have found that my patients appreciate seeing, as well as hearing, what needs to be done.'

'And Anthony admired your art work?'

'I'm no artist, Mr Prime Minister, though I understand you are. It was a simplified medical drawing, nothing more. After studying it, Mr Eden said he grasped things more fully.'

Moran cut in.

'Is his condition very critical?'

'It is, sir. If you'll excuse the expression I think there's little gas left in the tank.'

'Poor Anthony.'

'He may well become a chronic invalid.'

The Prime Minister walked a few paces away from his desk, with his head lowered, then asked,

'You mean I may have to relieve him of his duties?'

'Yes. If, that is, he survives, Prime Minister.'

'If he survives! What a grim thought. I am a gambling man, Dr Cattell. Despite Lady Churchill's disapproval, I like the gaming tables. Give me the odds on Mr Eden.'

'I am not a gambling man, sir. I am a Quaker.'

'That is of course to your credit. But imagine for a moment, if you would, imagine that on one wicked day of your otherwise exemplary life you spin the roulette wheels at Monte Carlo. The odds, Dr Cattell, if you will.'

The American did not like this one bit. He did not like English facetiousness, he had always found it a tiresome trait. He had always found English flippancy tiresome too.

'I do not deal in odds, Mr Prime Minister.'

The Prime Minister slowly walked back and forth across the room. The two doctors waited until he was ready. He looked an old man ageing further with every stride, a very tired old man looking out of the window on to the garden of Number 10. The sun was shining, and that did not help the Prime Minister one jot. When he next spoke it was to utter one word, and it was delivered without turning round.

'Charles?'

Moran, clearing his throat, addressed himself to Cattell.

'When can you do it?'

'Once he is fit to fly, and just as soon as I can reschedule my list.'

The Prime Minister's voice overrode Lord Moran's as they both immediately said:

'Fit to fly?'

'Yes. Strong enough to cross the Atlantic and strong enough to undergo a lengthy operation.'

'But you will operate here.'

'No, Mr Prime Minister, I will see the Foreign Secretary in Boston, so that I have my team with me. And my instruments. It could take up to six hours.'

'That is not a problem, is it, Charles? We will pay for your team and your instruments to come to London. I need Mr Eden in London. The operation must, I insist, take place in London. Indeed I need to consult, to confer, with him on a daily basis.'

The American spoke slowly and evenly.

'I'm afraid I will only operate on Foreign Secretary Eden in my own clinic.'

The Prime Minister, his cheeks a little flushed, was now back behind his desk, pressing on it with both hands.

'During the war, Dr Cattell – you may not know this – during the war, King George, in grave danger, was operated on while lying on the kitchen table in Buckingham Palace. And he made a complete recovery.' He banged the desk for his emphatic repeat:

'A *com-plete* recovery!'

'I am sure King George was a brave man.'

'He was. And he made no fuss.'

'What, may I ask, was the procedure?'

Moran averted his eyes as he snapped out the word:

'Appendicectomy.'

Dr Cattell stood up.

'I am sure, gentlemen, that you have surgeons in your great country who are extremely skilled in every emergency and more than capable to help Mr Eden through this trauma.'

Lord Moran stood up as well. There was a silence. The two Englishmen looked at the American. The American looked steadily at Sir Winston, holding his eye.

'Oh, all right,' the Prime Minister said. 'As you wish. We will do it the American way. And I shall tell President

Eisenhower how grateful I am to you when I meet him in a few weeks' time. Your name, Dr Cattell, will be on everyone's lips.'

'May I ask where you and the President will be meeting, sir?'

'In Bermuda. For our summit of the Big Powers. In Bermuda.'

The Prime Minister came round to shake Dr Cattell's hand, and did not immediately release it.

'So, Dr Cattell, it is America to the rescue. You win *again*! Our American friends now lead and we, it seems, must follow, cap in hand. A new world order is being established in all things, in all things political, military and medical. But nothing must go wrong in Boston.'

'I trust not, Sir Winston.'

'You will be saving the life of one of the most important men in the world, not to mention the next Prime Minister. You do know that?'

'You may be sure we will do our best.'

Sir Winston took Cattell's arm and eased him a little further away from Lord Moran.

'And did you also know that my mother was born in Brooklyn? Did you know, Dr Cattell, my mother was an American?'

The Prime Minister's eyes were red and moist.

'Then, sir, you had the best possible start in life.'

'I did indeed. I adored my mother. Adored her.'

*

Cattell turned to his swab nurse, his eyes narrowing as he went about his business.

'Retractor, please.'

Cattell knew better than anyone that botching surgery was nothing new and certainly not confined to incompetent Brits. In the Lahey Clinic he had often been, as a matter of urgency, called upon to do serious repair work. Over the years he had also found any number of things left inside the patient from an earlier operation, including sponges, a surgical instrument and, once, a towel with the name tag of the offending New York hospital clearly visible on it.

'Swab, please.'

Such was his fame, Cattell was often watched from the gallery by a dozen or more masked and gowned men. He was used to it, used to the theatre of the operating theatre. In 1953 the world travelled to Boston to see how he did it.

Cattell was now the cutting edge.

'The Cat' they called him.

'Cattell the Cat'.

'El Rapido'.

And for his anatomical accuracy, the range of his talent and his touch of genius, he was known in the clinic as 'Michelangelo'. They all wanted to see the Renaissance Man at work, and who could blame them.

Fatigue was not a word Cattell knew. As he sometimes reeled off three operations in a morning, the numbers who observed him were very high and increasing rapidly each year. Though unwilling to create any folklore about himself and the last man to play to any gallery, if other surgeons and other patients were to benefit in the future he did not mind the growing level of attention. At the start of our professional life, he said, we are all learner drivers. His allegiance was to medicine.

'Adjust the light, please.'

For Cattell medical science, particularly surgical practice, was partly about helping each other. Most unusually, he also allowed a smaller number to follow him around right there on the floor of the operating room, close enough to his big shoulders, leaning over to marvel at the unhurried speed of those strong wrists and long fingers and, above all, at his unruffled response in any crisis.

Watching Cattell and his scrub nurse work together on Mr Eden was like watching a dance. They glided.

'Clips. Scissors.'

They were like two practised and polished ballroom partners responding instinctively to each other's moves and prompts, anticipating each other's needs and movements, with barely a word passing between them, just a nod here or the flick of an eye there, knowing exactly what was wanted, if a quick change of step or a radically different approach was called for, the right instrument or suture always ready, his eyes and his hands never moving from their central purpose, and hers perfectly complementing them.

Dancers, that's what they were. Life-savers and dancers.

But on 23 June 1953 Dr Cattell had insisted no one

should be allowed in to observe. Not a soul. There would be just his team and the British Foreign Secretary on the table.

The gallery was to stay empty.

*

Nurse Appleyard liked things plain. Which was just as well given her small room at the very top of Chartwell, a room she reached up the steep back staircase. She had been plainly brought up: simple food, fresh air, hard work, a firm bed and a proper night's sleep. With the Appleyard family there was no money left for extras, and little time for those who demanded them. Don't hanker after everything, Millie, her mother said, be content with what you've got, love. Having things isn't the point, her father liked to say as he mended the puncture on her bicycle or put the chain back on. Possessions isn't the big issue, our Millie. Big issue today is the H-bomb.

So, accepting the regime of a nurse's life came fairly easily to Nurse Appleyard. She knew all about living in a nurse's cramped quarters and being on nights as well as on days. She also knew how to travel light. There were, however, a few personal touches she had slipped into her small suitcase. A framed snap of Mum and Dad with her in her swimsuit on Scarborough beach the year before they came south. The blue silk scarf given her by Gran for her twenty-first birthday. And the last letter she had ever received from Grandad, written in his copperplate. She went nowhere without that.

As for Arthur, he had recently given her a photograph of himself and she did think of bringing that along too, but decided against. She wouldn't tell him where she was going, she couldn't, which really annoyed him, and now she was not even sure she wanted to see him again. For one thing he was pressing her too hard. And if she wasn't sure about him in that area it was a bit half-baked putting up his photo on her bedside table. She didn't need to show off that she had a boyfriend, as some of the nurses felt obliged to do, and anyway there was no one at Chartwell to show off to, was there?

Before she had been allowed to settle into her room, she had been interviewed and instructed by Lady Churchill and then painstakingly checked out by Mr Colville. Every kind of ruler was passed over her. But from the moment she fetched up at the big gates she felt that even being there was a privilege, especially on a secret assignment to help the Prime Minister, even if it proved to be no more than alleviating pain and moderating sorrow.

Nurse Appleyard was told she would never, ever be able to tell a soul what she was doing. Matron had made that clear before she left the hospital. And she never would. Never ever. That was not a problem. She would not ask questions and she would keep her mouth shut. It was a bit like the poster back in the war which Dad still had pinned up in his shed. *Careless talk costs lives.*

Above all there was to be no mention, not even within the house itself, of the word *stroke.* She had been told that twice by Mr Colville, even though she had presumably been selected for her tact as well as her nursing. Indeed there was to be no mention of the Prime Minister being in bed at all. The Prime Minister was at Chartwell, in his country home. That was all. The Prime Minister was staying at his country home during the summer break, as he often did, and that was all anyone needed to know. No loose tongues from the staff, no foot and mouth outbreak, no idle talk in the Westerham pubs, otherwise some reporter from the *Daily Mirror* would be wriggling under the fence, with his ear close to the ground, or poking his binoculars through the high hedge.

And if she ever felt she was missing the banter and camaraderie of life on the ward, she had only to remember how much better the Chartwell food was than the hospital mince and mashed carrots, and if that didn't work she merely had to open the window in her room.

Just undo the latch and look out.

What a view!

Imagine living in a place like this. Well, she *was* living in a place like this, wasn't she? It took your breath away. This view was a first, and Millie liked to collect her firsts. She looked hard in all directions, soaking it up. Straight ahead, over the lawns to the lakes. Then, to the right, over the lawns to the outhouses. And, leaning out a little, straight down below her to the large patio. She could see two men hard at work in the kitchen garden. There was also a man outside the back door, just standing there. Not in working clothes. He must be a detective.

In the other direction was the wood. She recognised the lime trees. Her dad had told her about oaks and beeches and elms and limes. Trees weren't as easy to identify as birds, nowhere near, but she was getting there. When she had a bit of money to spare she must buy a guide book on trees.

Yes, Chartwell was another first for Millie. She had added a Prime Minister's home to the other firsts she had collected, the firsts which for one reason or another she would never forget. Her first injection, given with trembling hands. The sight of her first motorcycle accident, and the lad with a leg missing. Best of all the first birth she had attended, and worst of all, without a doubt, the first baby, with arched back, she saw die. Yes, there had been tears, but she would never be ashamed of tears. It's when you stop crying you're in trouble.

And now Chartwell.

One other reason that Nurse Appleyard travelled light was that she always lugged a heavy-ish book with her. *The Works of Jane Austen, Complete and Unabridged in One Volume.* It was an American edition (1942), all 1364 pages of it: Americans seemed to like their books big and long, didn't they, like their films. Wouldn't it be good to sail right across the Atlantic and see America for herself – America, where Jenny Smith had gone after she ran away from nursing to a new life.

But then Jane Austen was English, wasn't she, and she was proud of that, like the Brontë sisters were English, and she'd been on a day trip with her mother to Haworth to see the Brontë parsonage. She got her reading habit from her mother. They were both great readers.

*

They assembled in the faint perfume of Lady Churchill's sitting room just inside the front door: Clementine, Lord Moran and the Prime Minister's secretary. Colville made a little dramatic ritual of looking around for possible intruders and then securely closing the door. They remained standing.

'In the car, Jock?' the doctor asked.

'Yes, well before Westerham, in fact well before we got to Kent. He was fine at the start of the journey, developing a point as we were leaving Number Ten.'

'I already know this,' Clementine said.

'And what point was that?'

'Does it matter what the point was?'

For God's sake, woman! nearly slipped out. It was as much as Moran could manage simply to keep his temper with her.

'Clementine, I am trying to establish the general level of his articulation, of his lucidity, since he had the stroke. Please bear with me. What was he saying, Jock?'

'That he was the only survivor of the Big Three, now that Stalin had passed away, and he was going to stretch out his hand to grasp the Russian paw.'

'Oh, not the Russian paw again. The Russian paw!'

'Clementine.'

'We've heard that one before, a thousand times.'

'I would ask you again to give me a minute—'

Clementine was, however, not to be stopped, though her eyes were pleading.

'But he walked to the car, didn't he, Jock? After he'd stupidly gone ahead and taken the Cabinet. He walked quite well, I saw him out of the door.'

'Yes,' Colville agreed, 'otherwise I'm sure there would have been eyebrows raised, not to mention the press buzzing.'

'Could we *please*,' Clementine snapped at Colville, 'not talk about the press for one moment!'

'Of course. Forgive me. But he did give me the most strict instructions, before he became unclear, that no one was to know that he was temporarily incapacitated.'

'His words?' Moran asked.

'His words? That "the administration was to function as if he was in complete control". His exact words.'

'And when he arrived here?'

Colville looked at Lady Churchill before glancing at Moran, then, looking at his feet, he quietly said,

'He couldn't speak. He found it difficult to move his left leg and arm. And we had to carry him in. Thank heavens for the new nurse. She rather took over.'

'Being shaken about in the car won't have helped.'

'Rufus was terribly put out,' Clementine said with a high, almost hysterical laugh, followed by a gulp and tears.

'Rufus?'

'The poodle,' Colville whispered.

They waited for Clementine to recover.

'So,' Clementine said, pressing her handkerchief to her eyes, 'what are you going to do?'

'First things first. I'll speak to Nurse Appleyard. How's she going, by the way?'

'Very efficient in my view,' Colville said. 'No complaints so far.'

'She seems very self-contained,' Clementine said. 'And they like her in the kitchen.'

'I know the matron at Reigate well, and I told her I wanted the best nurse she'd got, no questions asked.'

'Winston loves being petted, as we all know, particularly by young gels.'

'And he'll need a wheelchair,' Moran said.

*

Whenever he was exhausted from the relentless strain of office, Winston was prone to say to his doctor, 'I want to sleep for a billion years, Charles,' and from the look of him he now well might be granted his wish. He was very still. There had been no need to knock on his bedroom door as the Prime Minister was quite unable to answer, but Moran did knock, and waited a civilised second or two before letting himself in.

A small bedroom for a great and courageous man.

Pulling up a chair at his old friend's bedside Moran could see immediately the deterioration in his patient over the last twenty-four hours. He was very pale, dense and heavy-limbed. There was a puzzled, almost aggrieved, frown on Winston's face, as if he was raising an eyebrow at this latest blow. His dignity was offended. His eyes were closed but not in peace. He was unreconciled. Worse, much worse, he seemed a long way off, in another place.

He breathed in.

And . . .

He breathed out.

But would he rally? Would he come back from the brink?

It was impossible for Moran to tell but, on balance, it seemed unlikely. Medicine and drugs could only do so much. There might be paralysis, with a lingering left side droop. The Prime Minister had all the tenacity required for a sustained recovery, oh yes, all of that and a lot more besides. But there was rhetoric and there was reality. Moran had seen him the worse for wear, had seen him befuddled, had seen him feverish with a high temperature, had seen him close to addled, but he had never seen him quite like this.

But then again you could not measure him, could you, against other men in similar circumstances? The Old Man wasn't like other men.

Moran sat back and exhaled slowly. And listened.

Churchill breathed in.

And . . .

Churchill breathed out.

For the moment the Prime Minister was still with them.

If he came round, though, if he pulled through, would he be different, altogether diminished? Would he be less than half the man he had been, a husk? What if that wonderful elasticity of mind could not be recovered, that gift for handling words and shaping sentences and stirring hearts. That unmatched ability to marshal words, to mobilise them and to send them into battle. And could that body, so used to absorbing punishment and coming back for more, could that constitution survive fifteen more rounds in the heavyweight ring, taking blows to the head and blows to the heart, slug it out and still be as it was before the latest life-threatening bout?

Was it folly to go on?

Was this the time for his corner, his doctor, to throw in the towel?

Hard to know.

Charles doubted he would ever again come across Winston beating time to the martial music coming out of his radiogram, or discover him singing (in his deplorable voice) 'The Soldiers of the Queen', or going on about stemming 'the Red Tide which is relentlessly rolling in from East to West'. Surely he had heard the last of all that.

Which reminded him . . .

Oh, sitting here he was reminded of all too much, of all too many Churchillian retorts and ripostes and random one-liners. They started to come to him thick and fast as the old doctor sat there, keeping his old friend silent company and giving him silent support. With Winston the present and the past always merged.

'And, Charles, that all came out of this poor nut.' That

was one Churchill liked to use, tapping his left temple, when he had been praised by Moran.

'I don't like flying through clouds, Charles. They may contain mountains.' A gloomy favourite of his when sitting next to his doctor on a long flight.

'I'm sorry, Charles, I'm not very amusing today.' That tended to be his first port of call as an apology, and a very unconvincing one, for being in a foul non-listening temper.

If pushed, on the evidence lying there next to him, Moran privately reckoned Winston would not last two days. Or, if he did survive, whatever his stock of courage, there could well be permanent brain damage. Not that he would dream of saying any such thing to Clementine. He would keep his counsel. He would grab at hope and put on the bravest face he could. Holding on to hope on the inside and putting on a brave face in public, that was the best course left open to the doctor.

Meanwhile . . .

His patient breathed in.

And . . .

His patient breathed out.

Time for a proper chat with the nurse.

*

Even the bravest know the birth of fear. Some soldiers are less windy than others, some less easily rattled. Some soldiers are blessed, if that is the right word, with a larger store of fortitude. But no one has an infinite amount of courage. Moran was sure of that.

And late one night a few years back – a dim, lamplit night, with two old men deep in their armchairs, two old comrades reminiscing together round the fire – he had tried to explain all this to Churchill, to give him the evidence on which his conclusions were based. But Churchill was uncomfortable with the topic: he smoked his cigar and looked at the embers in the grate and said,

'I don't give a fig what you yourself think as long as you keep all that psychiatric stuff out of the army, it might affect recruiting. Just because it's dirty weather you don't fold up. You have to stick at it. More life may trickle out of a man through thought than through a gaping wound, as Thomas Hardy said. Gloomy chap, mind you.'

And in an attempt to ensure the whole episode was closed the Prime Minister started to recite a bit of his favourite poetry:

Half a league, half a league,
Half a league onward,
All in the valley of Death . . .

Undeterred by Tennyson, Moran maintained that courage is like capital in the bank. Men start with different quantities and when it is spent then so are they. They are finished. Rest and recuperation may help a little, a brief respite away from the firing line may ease the anxiety, but no more than a little. Will power can only take you so far and should not be raised to the status of a super-human, godlike quality. Will power cannot stand alone on the podium. There is only so much petrol in the tank, only so much water in the deepest of wells, there are only so many buckets of courage even the bravest can dredge up.

Moran had more to say.

Put yourself in my shoes back in the trenches and tell me, Winston, how much shelling can this man stand? We've both been in the trenches. How many days and nights of relentless, constant bombardment and random sniping can this or that man endure? Moran, the most observant of doctors, had looked into the eyes of shell-shocked men, men alone and shaking with their terror, and he asked Churchill those questions only once, but he often asked them of himself because he had come to know better than anyone that we all have a breaking point.

In 1945, nearly three decades after his three years in the trenches, Moran had published *The Anatomy of Courage*, based on the records he kept while a young medical officer in the 1st Battalion of the Royal Fusiliers. Charles was at Ypres, and other battlefields. Close up, he had found one battlefield and one field hospital very much like another. From 1914 until 1917, for over a thousand days, he was responsible for the health of over a thousand men. Danger, discomfort and disaster he saw at first hand, and he saw them day after day. We all snap, he thought, oh yes, sooner or later we all snap, but each morning on parade Moran found that he had to put that general observation on one side, to put psychology on one side and decide, somehow decide, on the specific case before him: was this man genuinely ill or scrimshanking, was this soldier genuinely shell-shocked or just windy?

In his private diary Moran was sensitive to these issues but he was very strict on parade, with a reputation for severity. As a young medic he had found himself, against his will, playing the role of investigating officer as well as judge and jury, and he often sent men back to the front. Sometimes – and he still was haunted by this at three in the morning – sometimes he had made misjudgements, errors, fatal errors. Was he now – by encouraging, by even countenancing, Churchill's return to the political front line in his seventy-ninth year – making the biggest diagnostic mistake of his life?

Moran also knew, war aside, that there were many kinds of courage. Identifying physical courage, as displayed on the sports pitch, where you could see a lily-livered funk a mile off, the chap who wouldn't risk injury in the tackle, that was easy, but there was moral courage and the capacity to endure, both of which were much more difficult to spot. Not to mention what Napoleon called three in the morning courage: that was a rare form of courage indeed, perhaps the rarest, the resolve to face up and to see things through when you feel at your lowest and most vulnerable, when your spirits hit rock bottom and self-pity settles corrosively on your soul, those nights when you feel small and alone and below the level of events, those long hours when dawn never seems to come.

*

It wasn't just the way Jock Colville pronounced 'off' as *orf* or 'often' as *orfen,* though that tested one's patience, nor the fact that he knew or was connected to everyone from the young Queen down. It was the manner of his dress. How well pressed his trousers were, how well polished his shoes – look at the toe-cap shine – look at the cut of his suit jacket and the absolutely required amount of his shirt cuff that it revealed. Every component, every aspect was just so. In his manner of dress (as well as in the manner of his address) some in Westminster likened Jock Colville to the restrained and dignified Mr Darcy in *Pride and Prejudice,* not that Moran could see any similarity.

Chartwell was sombre, and it had been a mostly silent luncheon until, over coffee, the Prime Minister's secretary, dabbing his mouth with his napkin, turned to the Prime Minister's doctor, saying,

'I've been mulling something over, Charles, and Chartwell could really help us with this one.'

'Oh, yes,' Moran said, with the enthusiasm of a man who did not make conversation, 'which one is that?'

'With the newspapers, I mean. What line should one take?'

'In what way?'

'For our next move, I mean, after you've put out your short medical bulletin.'

'I'm working on the wording now. After that, what else is there to say?'

'One line of thought would be to write to Beaverbrook, Bracken and Camrose.'

Beaverbrook, Bracken and Camrose, the giants of Fleet Street!

'Tell the daily papers?' Moran snapped back.

'Not in so many words.'

'Tell all to the dirties?'

'No, of course not.'

'Are you mad?'

Colville raised his calming hand, allowing the smile he reserved for slow learners and cranky doctors.

'No, no. Put those three in the picture as soon as possible, fully and frankly, but *most* privately. Invite them in, very *entre nous*. As it were.'

'About the health of the Prime Minister?'

'Yes.'

'And Eden?'

'Precisely. Get the great barons down to Kent, invite the big beasts to Chartwell and appeal to their better natures, which it is possible they still possess. While mulling it over I was also thinking of writing a personal letter to each.'

'Why not telephone?'

'Too risky. Telephones *orfen* go wrong.'

'So do letters.'

'No, I plan to send a despatch rider, a private letter to each, asking them to come and see the Prime Minister. Well, as a matter of fact and to be perfectly frank I have already done so.'

'No point asking my opinion then, so here's a question for you. If things get worse, if the Prime Minister dies or is permanently incapacitated, and if, on top of that, Eden dies or is permanently incapacitated, who takes over?'

The Prime Minister's secretary put the points of his fingers together and looked slowly up at the ceiling, repeating the question as if slightly baffled.

'Who takes over?'

'Yes. If you can't gag the press. And if neither of them returns to full health you can't, can you? So who?'

Colville's tongue wetted his upper lip.

'It's a tricky question.'

'It is. So don't treat me as if *I* need a nurse as well.'

Arms crossed, they eyed each other, the unanswered question dismantling their brief rapport, each leaving the other guessing, each a bit miffed, each wishing the other would stick to his own last, stick to his own field of expertise, separate terrain. You to medicine, Charles, you to politics, Jock, and trespassers will be prosecuted. In other words, Keep Orf The Grass. With those close to Winston, however, with his particular ménage, with his attendant court, that was rarely on the cards.

'Could be a caretaker to hold the fort,' Colville said.

'Who?'

'Butler? Macmillan?'

'Macmillan?'

'Salisbury? We'll have to see what the Prime Minister says over the next few days.'

'Assuming he can say anything,' Moran countered. 'Assuming he isn't ga-ga. And he won't like being asked when he's going to die. People don't.'

*

Clementine Churchill was not alone in frowning upon diaries and diarists. Everyone did. Everyone was very candid indeed about how shocking and wicked diaries were. Disapproval, strong disapproval, was the party line. Diaries could create or dispel myths. They could expose or mislead. You could say anything in a diary, or into one of the new portable Dictaphones that were coming into use. For people close to power to be keeping a private daily record was considered at the very least poor form, not quite straight, and certainly not playing the game.

But the temptation to pick up a pen was strong, if not irresistible: that feeling in the fingers, that irresistible urge to jot down things that no one else knew let alone was supposed to talk about, things that must never, ever reach the public domain.

However tired or tetchy you were late in the evening, there was something deliciously clandestine about locking yourself in your room or your office or hotel room or embassy flat, then (when you were safely tucked away) unlocking a desk drawer, unscrewing your fountain pen, all this well out of the sight of your political masters, before starting to write in an unguarded manner. The moment felt ripe. There would be no fencing around the topic. The gloves were off and to hell with everyone. Instead of platitudes like 'Had a useful lunch and agreed to redouble our efforts with the Russians', you could say (and oh what a joy it was to speak so) 'X is a bumptious little shit and a slippery charlatan', or 'Y does like others to do all the dirty work for him. He'll go far.'

Lord Moran, Jock Colville and Evelyn Shuckburgh (Eden's private secretary) all kept diaries with varying degrees of discretion. Yes, it might be considered unethical. Yes, they might be breaking family confidences, if not in one case the Hippocratic oath. Yes, it was beneath them. Yes, they may have felt just a bit guilty as they unscrewed their pens, but they could not stop doing it, they really couldn't.

None of them knew for sure that the others were doing exactly the same, but as men of the world – and you could not attain such positions as they occupied without being a man of the world – each probably assumed the others were up to something.

'One for your diary, I think.'

'Or for yours.'

Did they aim to tell the unvarnished truth, or did they hope to appear – if ever they published – as rather more important even than they were? Not so much regular dinner guests, more than minor characters, more even than distinguished diplomats on the fringes of power, but central players, *confidants*, irreplaceable people in the know, men of shaping influence on the great stage.

Yes, there was something subversively thrilling and self-serving about this practice, and no one was better at it than the English, which was one reason why, all charm and sweet reason on the surface, they made such good spies. You could always silently revisit your diary and embed something you did not say the first time, or you could affect being garrulously rushed, giving an off-the-cuff impression, while in fact you were producing a skilfully polished and edited work of art.

Sometimes diarists drifted into even murkier waters, leaving controversial days completely blank only to return to them later, with the appropriate ink, return to fill in the gap with the benefit of hindsight to prove they had an infallible nose. In other words, retrospectively doctoring their own diaries.

*

Nurse.

Nurse?

Nurse!

After a few days Nurse Appleyard was already more than used to being summoned at any hour, day and night, often abruptly. It might be the doctor or Lady Churchill or Mr Colville. It had been like that from the very first moment. Any one of them might arrive at the Prime Minister's bedroom unannounced, like a jack in the box. But Nurse Appleyard was never caught off balance. She had very sharp hearing and she was always ready. Each visitor had a clearly different and characteristic footfall. Other footsteps, ones she did not yet recognise, flitted by or paused or hovered around outside the door. Were those the detectives?

Nurse!

She had, of course, been immediately sworn to secrecy

by Matron in her office before she left work at the hospital. And yet again, after she arrived at Chartwell, by Lord Moran. The doctor – Lord Moran, but she called him doctor – could be a bit curt and heavy-handed. He sometimes treated her as if she was a slip of a girl rather than an experienced young woman. But then senior doctors (and, come to think of it, some very junior ones) were often like that in hospitals, altogether too full of themselves, particularly before they got to know you.

Still, she was used to it. That was the way of the medical world, and no one in her world was more important than the President of the Royal College of Physicians. And here he was, Lord Moran, talking quietly to her outside the Prime Minister's bedroom.

'Could you make any sense of him this afternoon, nurse?'

'He's a bit muzzy, doctor, and it's hard to pick anything up. He tries to speak, then can't.'

'Nothing of note, then?'

'He did say one word.'

'What was that?'

'He said Burma a couple of times.'

'Bermuda, you mean.'

She did not retract.

'No, it was Burma. He was a bit hoarse, a bit muffled, but it was Burma.'

'Could have been Burma, I suppose.'

Because it might sound silly, the nurse felt she couldn't go on to add *the Prime Minister, although silent, almost speaks to me with his hands and his eyes.* She couldn't say that she had noted the shadow of a crooked smile on his mouth, that his eyes were more alive than his face and that, once, there was the hint of a nod, all signs that he seemed on the edge of something, of some kind of return.

She did not say any of that to the doctor because she could not prove it. But she was a good nurse, she knew she was, and single-minded, her father always called her that, and she trusted her instincts.

Moran looked more closely at Nurse Appleyard, taking stock of her. She was doing well. He could see no cause for complaint. She kept the Prime Minister's bed fresh, the kidney dishes were always clean and everything in the room was tickety-boo. She seemed a sensible enough girl, and she stood up for herself. Nothing timid about her. He approved of that. And there was something else, something about her that he warmed to.

'Are you from around here, Nurse Appleyard?'

'Yorkshire, sir, originally.'

'Ah, I thought I heard something. I am too. I was born in Skipton. We're both from Yorkshire then.'

'Skipton's nice, sir. Very nice. We're from Bradford.'

'That's very nice too.'

'Is it!'

They shared a nod and a smile.

'So what brought you to these parts?'

'We live down here now, doctor, not far from here, and have done for a while. My father came down south for a job, he had to, soon after the war. He lost his job and needed the work.'

'And what does he do, your father?'

'He runs a bicycle shop in Redhill. He repairs bikes. And sells them. Raleighs.'

'Very good bicycles, Raleighs.'

'Oh, my dad knows just about everything there is to know about Raleighs. He's now bought the shop.'

'And where did you train?'

'At St Bartholomew's, sir.'

'Bart's? Very good. Very good. Second best hospital in London.'

Her eyes sparked up.

'Bart's is second to none, doctor. That's what my parents were told, and so was I, and I believe it. I always wanted to train there and I worked hard and I did.'

'Good for you.'

He started to move away.

'You're doing well. Stay alert, Nurse Appleyard, and take any opportunity to ask the Prime Minister questions.'

'I will, doctor.'

'Who knows, he might wake up tomorrow as right as rain.'

'That would be grand, wouldn't it?'

She turned the bedroom door knob as quietly as possible. It squeaked. She stepped back inside, trying to make no sound as she crossed the floor. She was beginning to know his bedroom through her feet, the slight creak of her step as her weight went down, with something coming back up through her soles: she was beginning to think she could walk around his room blindfolded. As well as feeling her feet touching the floor she felt, as it were, the floor making its mark, leaving its imprint on her. She liked that. The more alive she was the more she could help those who were ill.

'Prime Minister? It's me. I'm back.'

She had quickly grown used to the place, to his private space, but at first she had thought it odd and disconcerting that Sir Winston and Lady Churchill had separate bedrooms. Did they not share a bed? Was it rude to ask if not, why not? Did they not love each other any more? Older people sometimes fell out of love. Did they never share a bed? Or was this how aristocrats lived, did they start the night in one bed and end up separately? The thought made her smile. And was it usual for the lady's bedroom to be so much bigger than the man's?

But wasn't it nice, if you were married, to go to sleep and to wake up in each other's arms? She had always felt that would be nice, having your husband's warm body next to yours, with his arm around you. It was a life she hoped to have and to share one day, not that she was getting any closer to it. Anyway, whichever way you looked at it, having different bedrooms was very odd and about as different as possible from her own family, all living cheek by jowl in their Redhill terrace with the barest minimum of privacy.

Still, Nurse Appleyard thought, we're all different, aren't we? As her dad liked to say, it takes all sorts, our Millie.

As her eyes gradually adjusted back to the Prime

Minister's bedroom, the half-light seemed to show up certain books in his bookcases and draw her towards them. Her hand reached out and she took one from the shelf at random and turned it over in her hands. She felt it and smelt it. It was surprisingly heavy, with leather binding and gold lettering. It smelt of old leather and glue. Then, with a guilty tremor at what she had done, she put it straight back.

Her heart was really going on.

She shouldn't have done that. Books were private. They were presents, they were gifts, things you owned and put your name in. They said something about you. You couldn't just take books off someone else's shelf like that without asking, least of all not off the Prime Minister's you couldn't. It was rude. It was a bit of a cheek. Her face was now a bit hot.

And they looked very serious, these books, all of them, leather bound and old. She wanted to know more about them. What kind of books did he read? She knew he was a writer as well, a proper author. Were any of his books made-up stories, were any of them novels, or were they all history? When he got better she would ask him. Knowing him, he had probably written quite a few of them in the room.

And did he like Jane Austen?

Of course he did.

Two days ago Lady Churchill had put a small vase of sweet peas, all different colours, on her husband's side table. The flowers stood in front of the photographs of their four grown-up children. At first Nurse Appleyard was not sure of the names of them all, but she had found that out from the housekeeper downstairs: they were Randolph, Sarah, Diana and Mary. And they lost a little girl, a little girl coming up for three. The housekeeper, who brought up the fresh bed linen each day, looked round and quietly mouthed *Mari-gold*. The one they lost was called Marigold.

Nurse Appleyard smelt the sweet peas. If there was a better smell in the world she didn't know it. She'd love a garden full of them. Not a huge garden like Chartwell, of course. It could be their small patch back at home. She'd settle for a back garden. She took out a few of the sweet peas that had gone limp and put them in the wastepaper basket. One fell apart and she picked up the tiny petals off the carpet.

On the shelf running along the other side of his bed was a bunch of heather recently sent by an admirer in Scotland. Imagine having admirers like that! Apparently small presents, often anonymous thank-yous, arrived for the Prime Minister all the year round. Imagine having unknown admirers and a large house with every room full of books. You wouldn't need to go to the public library.

She looked down on his face and touched the blotched skin on the back of his hand. She noticed he was having some difficulty swallowing. His mouth gawped. He was dribbling a little, too, from the left-hand corner of his mouth, a tiny rivulet running down a crease in his chin. With the lightest of touches she dabbed it dry.

'Can I get you anything?'

As a nurse she knew quite early on if she was going to have a rapport with a particular patient. It was hard to say why. With some patients you kept your distance; with some there was a natural warmth and ease. Although they had exchanged no words she sensed that she was going to get on with this man who was born in a palace and had shelves full of leather-bound books with gold lettering.

She brushed away a stray white hair from his face. His eyelids flickered as if he had sensed that touch. She sat down, as quietly as she could, at his side. She took his hand and held it until he was deeply asleep, then she gently loosened her fingers.

Tonight she would pray for him.

*

It was Shakespearean. Or it had at least its Shakespearean side. It was, Jock Colville felt as he saw them settle around the table, not unlike one of those scenes in the cycle of history plays which they used to read around the class at Harrow. *Henry IV Part One*, *Henry IV Part Two*, and *Henry V*. There were three lords – it was usually three and you could hardly tell them apart – who gathered together, often secretly, often conspiratorially, sometimes at odds with one another, to discuss what they were going to do next about their tyrannical or absent or slowly dying king. How were they going to 'hit together'?

Here they come.

Enter the Earl of Worcester; Harry Percy (Hotspur); and the Earl of Northumberland

or

Enter Richard, Earl of Cambridge; Lord Scroop of Masham; and Sir Thomas Grey, Knight of Northumberland

or, as here,

Enter

(i) Lord Beaverbrook (Max Aitken, seventy-four, originally from Canada, Minister of Aviation Provision in the Second World War)

(ii) Viscount Camrose (William Berry, also seventy-four, originally from Wales, Merthyr Tydfil in fact, who was once diddled over a newspaper deal by the man on his left, Max Beaverbrook)

(iii) Viscount Bracken (originally from Ireland, via Australia, Minister of Information in the Second World War. Now aged fifty-four, though as an unruly red-headed schoolboy at Sedbergh he had pretended to be three years younger than he was).

Not that these three lords now around the table at Chartwell, whatever their pasts, were disloyal rebels hatching an insurrection or planning an assassination. Far from it. They were, in their differing ways, huge Winston fans, absolutely devoted to the Old Boy; the good-natured Camrose had even played a central role in purchasing Chartwell and presenting it to the National Trust on the condition that Churchill, to whom the country owed so much, should have it as his home for the rest of his life.

But it was, nonetheless, a plot of a kind that Colville was

now advocating, and the three men who were being asked to rally to his help added up to a massively influential group of magnates. Before they arrived Jock Colville had, to cheer himself up, written down on the left-hand side of a piece of paper exactly which newspapers they owned.

He enjoyed doing this:

The Daily Express
The Sunday Express
The Economist
The Banker
The Financial News
The London Evening Standard
The Daily Telegraph
The Sunday Times

Quite a line-up. A bit of firepower there.

Colville was leading on to the pitch a pretty strong team, men who could make or break you, or rather he was hoping to persuade his top team not to run on to the pitch at all: in fact, to lie doggo in the changing room. Recently Jock had found himself rather enjoying these football analogies. We in Britain are inside right, America is outside right; Russia is inside left, China outside left, and so forth.

The three men had all been driven to Chartwell separately, soon after dusk, Camrose arriving last, and the first thing each of them asked of Lady Churchill was the health of the Prime Minister. Was there any improvement? What was the latest state of play? The second thing they asked was to be allowed to see their dear old friend, the stricken warrior. Lady Churchill, who had very little time for his cronies, particularly for the 'two terrible Bs' (as she called them), politely replied that unfortunately a bedside visit to her husband was not possible. He was very poorly, doctor's orders and all that.

Not that the doctor (coming down the stairs to shake their hands) had ordered it exactly, but common sense advised against any demands being made of his patient, and privately he was not even sure Winston would survive the week-end. Rest. Total rest, and pray hard that he would turn the corner. That's what the doctor ordered.

Moran knew the terrible Bs very well, Camrose less so. Indeed Beaverbrook and Bracken, both patients of his, had recommended to Churchill, when he became Prime Minister in 1940, that Charles Wilson (as he then was) should become his personal physician. Beaverbrook had written to Moran urging him to carry that burden: 'Now, good doctors in the world are few, and you are the best of them all. The most honest, the most simple, the most clever and the most upright.'

Furthermore, for many years Max Beaverbrook had been a large benefactor and generous fund-raiser for Moran's beloved St Mary's Hospital (where Moran had been a long-serving Dean), so they had seen a fair bit of each other, warts and all, and many of his critics who had seen him close up reckoned that there were plenty of warts on Beaverbrook.

A maid knocked and came in with a tray of sandwiches. Colville had already lined up the port, the whisky, the brandy and the soda siphon.

'Would you like me to join you?' Moran asked.

'I think we can manage on our own, Charles, thank you,' Colville said.

*

While Moran stewed in his room, and wrote up his diary with an irritably quick hand, Colville chaired the meeting.

'Gentlemen, I'm grateful to you for coming down to Kent at the end of a long day. I do know you're all very busy men.'

'Least we could do.'

'Don't mention it.'

'And I was wondering if first of all we could be very clear about our purpose in gathering together.'

Beaverbrook poured himself a brandy, speaking as he did so:

'No need for all that, Jock. We know why we're here. You want us to gag our patch.'

'I think I'm saying that such an approach would be in the national interest.'

'Sit on it. Same thing. No Winston, no Eden, no one on the bridge, so keep mum. Mum's the word.'

'But what happens if the *Mirror* sniffs something and steals a march on us?'

'Bloody rag.'

'But read by an awful lot of people.'

'But they don't *know*, do they? And the idea is that we keep it that way.'

'Has the Cabinet been informed, Jock?'

Colville paused before saying,

'Yes, Butler has told them. Only the barest minimum. And it wasn't minuted.'

'But not Parliament of course?'

'There are, as far as I know, no plans to tell Parliament either now or in the future.'

While they all sat absorbing that, Bracken lit a cigarette and reached a hand out for the port. Camrose, who always liked to take the long view, broke the silence, raising his glass, and speaking for the first time.

'Before we go any further, a toast. To Winston.'

'Winston.'

'Winston. God bless him.'

'And our country.'

'And our country.'

'And because it is Winston, and because it is our country, it is our privilege and our duty to mind our own business on this matter.'

'Well said, William.'

'Indeed, in my view we have no option.'

'There's always an option.'

'It's high summer and the silly season for news. We've climbed Everest and there's all to play for in the Ashes.'

'I didn't know you liked cricket, William.'

'I don't, Max, but I can see its political virtues. And we have the Christie murder trial, and sentencing coming up.'

'Plenty of lurid details there to keep them happy.'

'More of the same, then.'

It was all going so well, perhaps almost too well, that Colville wondered if they were guarding their hands and playing poker. They were, after all, turning their backs on a huge scoop and a big splash. They were being asked to ignore sales figures, to ignore circulation. Barely moving his head, Jock looked carefully from face to face around the table to see what, if anything, he could read there. Reading people, reading their motives, was something Colville liked to do.

Beaverbrook.

Bracken.

Camrose.

Was he seeing loyalty or vanity in their expressions, was he witnessing a sense of decency or mere self-importance? He wanted to know but there was no way he could be sure.

'So the whole world and his dog knows Eden is in hospital?'

'I wouldn't quite say that, Brendan.'

'More to the point, how many know about Winston? What's the tot-up?'

'The Cabinet. And the immediate household here. That's all.'

'And us.'

'And us indeed.'

'That's fine by me.'

'And me.'

'As long as it stays that way.'

'The only circulation that matters at the moment is the Prime Minister's.'

'Good headline, that.'

'If one we will never run.'

'Is there going to be a medical bulletin of any sort, Jock?'

'Charles is working on that as we speak. At least I trust he is.'

'What are you going to say?'

'Something low key and dignified, that's what we're after, something that ensures we have a measure of control.'

'Don't move a muscle, then? Parliament doesn't have a clue and we conceal the truth?'

'Another brandy, Max?'

*

'Mr Eden, how are you this morning, sir?'

A gaunt and sluggish Eden gave a weary smile. His cheeks were sunken, his throat was parched and the middle of his dry bottom lip was cracking open.

'I am very well. Thank you.'

'Everything went as we hoped. Everything is as we expected. We are very pleased with your general progress. All the signs are positive.'

Eden smiled wearily again.

'That is good news.'

The repairs to his common bile duct had been carried

out to plan. While no one was suggesting the immediate future would be a bed of roses, Dr Cattell reassured Mr Eden that, given the necessary time and the necessary patience, there was every prospect of a full recovery and his return, in due course, to normal life and to his demanding schedules.

'Thank you. I can ask for no more.'

Dr Cattell did not wish, however, to put a firm date on the timing of that recovery. Indeed he could not. Let us, Mr Foreign Secretary, see what the future brings. Meanwhile Sir Winston and the British government must accept the facts. Mr Eden, in his present condition, was strongly advised to remain in the clinic for a week, then to convalesce fully in the city of Boston and so rebuild his strength for at least three weeks, four would be better, before even contemplating the journey across the Atlantic home.

'Of course. I accept your advice and will do whatever you deem best.'

Dr Cattell concluded the consultation by informing Mr Eden that he would, before the day was out, as specifically requested by the British government, be sending a formal and detailed report on the Foreign Secretary's medical condition to Prime Minister Churchill in London. (Little did he know that the Prime Minister's own medical condition ruled him out of reading anything.) In this report Dr Cattell would chart every step the hospital had taken since Mr Eden was admitted to their care, while – and this he would not say – omitting any mention, let alone admonition, of the unmitigated shambles left by the English surgeons.

Mr Eden went to shake Dr Cattell by the hand but in doing so found himself constrained by various tubes and drips connected to his right wrist.

'Dr Cattell,' Mr Eden said, 'I am deeply grateful to you all, but to you in particular for your expertise and—'

'Sir, it was an honour. I was proud to be asked to help a great ally of our country. So were my fine team here at the Lahey Clinic.'

'Will you pass on my heartfelt thanks to all those who assisted you?'

'You may be assured I will.'

And with that the surgeon walked swiftly away, his hammer toes hurting, his long legs eating up the corridor back to his office. Within the hour Dr Cattell had begun another procedure.

*

As Nurse Appleyard opened the Prime Minister's bedroom curtains, not long after dawn, she spotted some men pacing the lawns below. She looked again, this time more carefully. She had never seen them before. There had been no visitors since she had arrived, or none that she herself had passed around the place, and yet here were three strangers on the lawn. But she knew there was no cause for alarm. Intruders would not be walking around in full view like that. And there were detectives in the house.

Even so it was early, very early, to be out there. Normally she might see one of the gardeners doing some watering of the flower beds before the summer sun became too warm, but these men in dark suits must have either driven up at the crack of dawn or slipped into the house very late last night. She had, though, heard no cars coming and going. Something about these distant figures suggested that (in one of her father's phrases) they were 'top men'.

One was taller than the other two. The smallest was waving his hands around as if conducting an orchestra or a brass band. The one in the middle was quite fat. Every ten yards or so they paused, formed a close little huddle, then once more moved on.

Turning back to Sir Winston she lifted up the sheet at the bottom of his bed and looked again at his feet. She took out the hot water bottle, now barely warm. His feet felt cold and heavy and unresponsive. She doubted the hot water bottle was doing any good. She wondered, could she help improve the circulation in his lower calves, ankles and feet by moving and manipulating and massaging them? She had tried it before on wards with the bed-bound elderly, those with hardening arteries who had muscular pains or bad attacks of cramp or numbness or restless legs. Often they were overweight patients who smoked a lot or who had socks that were too tight. Any number of things could, she knew, choke the blood supply. She found that massaging and flexing and 'working' their feet sometimes encouraged better blood flow and improved their chances of walking again.

And at the very least her touch seemed to make them

feel better. When the doctor was next in an amenable mood she would broach the idea and see how it went down.

Ten minutes later, with Sir Winston still inert on the bed, she took another look out of the window and there they still were, the three men in dark suits, still pacing up and down the same part of the lawn, only now it was the tall one who was doing the gesticulating. The other two leant towards him, listening.

This time they did not move on but nodded and all shook hands.

*

Whenever Clementine came to peep at him, to check up on him or to stay a while with him, Nurse Appleyard tiptoed out. When Clementine came to leave his room after her private time, the nurse would slip back in, an unobtrusive figure barely noticed by Lady Churchill were it not for Nurse Appleyard's smile, and what a smile, of open encouragement.

During that most dangerous period, when all was in the balance – during those voluble days of endless questions downstairs, repeatedly begging reassurance from Charles, begging with a beat missing in her heart, hugging herself in those dead hours of the night and those dumbstruck dawns – Clementine went through the whole gamut of emotions, every high and every sheer drop.

She flicked a dead fly off the bedroom windowsill. Then she turned and sat, watching her husband's eyelids flick and flutter. Was trouble brewing, was his breathing too shallow? She was worried when his lungs made a sound and worried when they did not. Suddenly she was seething with anger at what he had so foolishly done to himself and to her and to her hopes for their future, before lurching into overwhelming tenderness, muffled tears and sudden hugs, one minute fearful as the choked phlegm caught in the back of his throat, the next moment relieved as he swallowed and settled, galloping concern followed by stiffening resolve to see him better again, to see him laugh again, to watch him light up a cigar again, to see him up on his pins again even if there was a waddle in his walk, to hear once more the summer sound of mallet on ball, as every fluctuation of love and fear in her tightened or loosened its grip with the onset of the other.

Oh no, the gamut of emotions, that tired old phrase, didn't begin to catch it at all. The gamut wasn't the half of it.

Clementine also bitterly reflected on what was going on outside his bedroom, beyond the walls of Chartwell and the Weald of Kent, up in Westminster, in the wider world of politics. The world of politics where words were polished and glibly spoken or deviously unsaid in a polished way, lies flying on their own wings, the decorous knavery, the sleight of tongue, the endless talk about Winston, the Winston chat, the muttering collision of Winston myths and the shackling mesh of Winston anecdotes.

People could go on for ever about Winston. And they

did. And it seemed that is exactly what they would continue to do, as long as he himself went on for ever, as long as he himself continued to believe that no one else in the world could rotate the globe in their hands quite as he did. It all made her want to scream. It made her want to pummel her head on the pillow and cry out, 'Yes, but he's just an old man, a tired old man, with his batteries run down. He's gone to the dogs. Let me be plain. The big bonfire is down to ash. Enough is enough! It's as simple as that.'

But of course it wasn't as simple as that. Nothing ever was, because Winston had chosen this life of his and even as he lay there it seemed he, infuriatingly, was willing his body to go on. Willing the old carcass, as he called it, in that hateful phrase of his, willing himself to fight the good fight with all his might. It was maddening. She might rage at Charles, she might complain to Jock and the others, she might hate his newspaper cronies, she might be infuriated by his whole entourage, but she knew where it all started and where it all ended: with Winston himself. He often said that it fitted him, this role on the world stage, like the old scuffed slippers he loved to wear.

After another restless night, Clementine put on her dressing gown and her slippers and left her bedroom. It was just turning light on the close-cropped lawns of Chartwell. With only the earliest of birds singing, she passed through his study.

Half way across the study something stopped her. She looked round in alarm and listened. There was no sound, nothing untoward, nothing. But she knew what it was. It was as if more of him was now in here than was lying in the bedroom. It was here in the study that he researched and wrote his early drafts, surrounding himself with reference books, often standing for hours at his lectern as he did so, or pacing up and down dictating to one of his secretaries. Standing next to the globe, writing. In this room, Winston, you stood right there at the lectern, for weeks and months on end, lost in the past, and often oblivious of me.

Here he had written his huge biography of Marlborough, and later the six volumes of *The Second World War*:

The Gathering Storm
Their Finest Hour
The Grand Alliance
The Hinge of Fate
Closing the Ring
Triumph and Tragedy

She moved on. As she came close to his bedroom door she felt a small clutch of pain.

She went inside. With Nurse Appleyard a quiet sentinel sitting on her chair outside, Clementine spoke silently to her husband's rumpled and sleeping face, whispering her heart to heart.

'Winston dear, you sleep on, while I sit here and talk to you. You must rest. Rest for a long while. First, just to say that the Queen telephoned this evening. From

Scotland. She is starting her coronation tour of Scotland tomorrow. She is very sorry to hear about you and sends her very best wishes for your speedy recovery. Isn't that lovely of her? Also, I'm here now because I want to talk to you when you can't answer back. I'm sorry but I want to talk to you when you can't defeat me with your turns of phrase, and when you can't harangue me – as you sometimes can – or be bullying or bombastic. Everyone here wants you to recover, not just the Queen, everyone else in the country – if they only knew about it – would want you to recover, and I suspect you will get better, you're too strong to die.'

She pressed his hand.

'But we all want you to rest. Mary feels the same. All the children do … Sarah telephoned. Randolph, yes, Randolph has telephoned as well. No, he has, really. And this time he didn't blow his top. In fact he suggests you take a breather. Well, his exact phrase was *please urge Father to catch his breath for a bit.* And Diana. She was a bit nervy, and who can blame her? But you mustn't ask any more of yourself. Or me. Because the truth is I haven't the strength left. I'm going under, I'm puttering out, like an old candle. And I can't go on leaving any more little notes for you round the house. Because I'm not colluding any more.'

She felt the resentment rising.

'I've given everything to this life we lead, trailing and traipsing around as the years raced by and we lost track of the girls as they shot out of their frocks, and I barely noticed, no wonder that they've had their problems, because I've put absolutely all I've got into you, and we've paid for it, haven't we, we've paid hand over fist. We've been too prodigal. Overspilt. Overspent. You've achieved more than any man alive, much more, so please listen to me. Please. I mean really listen. Would you?'

Tears were not far away.

'You promised Anthony in the war. Ten years or more ago. You wrote to the King saying that in the event of your being killed in an aeroplane, on one of your long freezing cold flights, he should send for Anthony. Anthony has been the most brilliant, the most loyal of men, and you know as well as I do that he is living in hope, living in that expectation. Recovering his health, in that expectation. You must, deep down, know that. You promised him again in 1950. I know you still regard him as a young man, but he isn't, he really isn't, and things have taken their toll on him as well. As for me, if my view counts, I did not want us to return to Downing Street in 1951, and you may remember I begged you not to. And a fat lot of good that did.'

She started to cry.

'And just look at the state of you now! Your head lolling. You can't bounce back from this one. With your mouth open and . . . '

She hurried out, bumping into this, bumping into that, back to her own bedroom.

*

There was no question of knocking. Moran barely saw the door for the red mist. He slammed the piece of paper down in front of Colville, who barely had time to slip his diary back in the drawer.

'Where is it?'

'What?'

'Where is *disturbance of the cerebral circulation*? That was the phrase I used for the bulletin. Where *is* it?'

'It's not there,' Jock said, without even looking at the bulletin.

'Why not? I am his doctor and I wrote it. And you accepted it.'

'It was felt to be too strong.'

'Too strong?'

'Politically too strong.'

'By whom?'

'By politicians.'

'By prima donnas, you mean.'

'We're talking about a press bulletin, Charles, that is all. We agreed with Beaverbrook, Bracken and Camrose that we had to put out *some*thing. And this is it.'

'We are talking of including the minimum of medical fact here. You and I agreed the wording, didn't we?'

'Yes.'

'And a *disturbance of the cerebral circulation* is exactly what the Prime Minister has. Not this bland nonsense. Not this piffle. *The Prime Minister has had no respite for a long time and is in need of a complete rest. We have therefore advised him to abandon his journey to Bermuda and to lighten his duties for a month.* If anything is likely to make the *Mirror* smell a rat it's that!'

'The redrafting was done by Mr Butler and Lord Salisbury.'

'Are they doctors now?'

'With Anthony in Boston it was their decision.'

'It is a suppression of the facts, as simple as that.'

'Others might see it as standing by our leader at a very difficult time.'

'Jock, listen to me, just for once. You think you are very clever. And in your own way you may be. But you're too quick to think your yea must be yea and your nay nay. No one who knows the Prime Minister will believe for one moment that he's taking a month's rest just because he's been overdoing it. He's been overdoing it all his life, for God's sake. You are taking a terrible gamble with this bulletin. I dissociate myself from it. Completely.'

'Charles, if you'll just bear with me a moment while I—'

'No, find yourself a political doctor.'

And he strode out of the front door and into the garden and set off on his walk.

*

Lord Moran had to walk, had to, had to.

His veins were bursting.

The walk would help. Bound to.

Even if it was the same walk.

Particularly if it was the same walk.

Routine, he needed routine. You couldn't live without routine.

He would set off at any time of the day – on a damp morning or a warm evening or (as here) on a dozy summer afternoon – because the satisfactions of exercise were well known to him and part of him was conscious, even in a foul temper, that he always returned to the house a little less incendiary.

Colville.

Col-*ville*!

Keep walking. You'll soon feel better. A good punishing walk will sort you out. As well as offering him respite from Colville and Clementine, who seemed somehow to hunt as a pair – if one of them didn't get you the other one would – the garden at Chartwell was more than big enough for Charles to stride out in. Furthermore, if he walked round the whole perimeter he found that not only did he soon recover his mood but it added up to an aromatic constitutional, particularly if you had Lord Moran's puritanical habits and did the circuit twice, or as he put it, took a couple of brisk turns around the park.

The thing he was perhaps most keen to escape, over and above the reprehensible fiddling with his medical bulletin, was being endlessly intercepted on the wooden staircase. Whether he was going upstairs or coming back down, day or night, he found himself being wedged in and challenged on his professional judgements: it happened after almost every sentence he spoke, challenges which came close to being affronts.

Then, as if that wasn't enough, the cheek, the barefaced cheek to start changing what he had written as a physician!

Keep walking.

Keep the deep breathing going.

Each hundred yards his anger lessened.

And he talked to himself.

Or, rather, gave himself a talking to.

You must not be rude. Dorothy had often told him straight: being candid was fine, but being rude was not. *You think you are very clever. And in your own way you may be.* Saying that to Jock Colville was going too far. He nodded to himself. Rude. And Colville had been brave in the war, very brave, he must not forget that. Only a brave man joined the RAF when he need not have done, only the bravest became fighter pilots, and Colville was rightly proud of dodging enemy flak and anti-aircraft fire in his Mustang.

Moran walked on.

As for Lady Churchill, he had to accept that Clemmie had every right to get into a bit of a flap or go off in an almighty huff if she wanted to, after all she'd been through. Any health problem with Winston was an arrow to her heart, to her heart more than anyone's. Her behaviour was more than understandable, and he must recognise that.

Moran started his angry circuit at the entrance lawn by the front door, and made his way anti-clockwise along the line of copper beeches, with birds abandoning their perches and darting out of the limes, then he skirted the croquet lawn (silent, no noise was allowed within earshot of Winston's bedroom) and dropped on down towards the outhouses and the studio (curiously padlocked now) where, in happier times, Winston painted away for hours on end.

If the doctor came across a gardener working with a length of twine or doing some raking or leaning on a spade, he might exchange a brief word, but it would be the briefest possible word. The most appealing pleasure of solitary walking for Lord Moran was precisely that it was solitary, i.e. that it preferably involved not having to open your mouth.

From the outhouses he continued on round the lower lake and the upper lake, with the two black swans and the skittering ducks mudlarking and the breeze lightly rippling the water. He paused for a few seconds to look up at the main house, warm brick, tall and wide, his eye picking out the dining room, the drawing room, the study, and then settling on the corner window of the small bedroom where the great man lay.

The curtains were drawn.

Nurse Appleyard would be up there.

A good nurse. A good Yorkshire lass.

Matron was right: she wasn't run of the mill.

He moved back up the gentle slope past the swimming pool, which Churchill had helped to build himself, round the corner of the shrubberies, towards the rose garden and goldfish ponds and the upper terrace. An added advantage of these walks was that if a crisis did occur he was, at least for much of the walk, visible from the house and could easily be summoned. He never was, and never wished to be, far away from his patient. It had been like that since he first became the Prime Minister's doctor in the dark days of 1940, and it would be like that until he, whichever he it was, died.

Striding briskly up the slope, with a song thrush nearby, Moran was suddenly reminded of rugger training in his school days at Pocklington. This was way back before the First World War, right, boys, twice round the pitch, no cutting corners, then twenty press-ups, proper press-ups, and you'll be running round the pitch again if I see any of you slacking. And you stragglers at the back better watch out, I've got my eye on you! It reminded him, too, of the time when he was captain of the St Mary's side himself and famed for his fearless tackling, but mostly it brought back later years, years of watching the St Mary's Hospital XV, his pride and joy, in the golden decade when they triumphed in the Hospital Cup six years in a row, largely because Moran as Dean was the unashamed driving force behind the hospital's entry policy.

That was another controversy.

In medical circles it had been rumoured that if they ever found themselves short of a scrum-half at St Mary's, the Dean would throw a rugby ball during the applicant's interview, and if you caught it you were accepted. Moran didn't deny the story. Why would he? He saw the story as a slap on the back not a slap in the face. He believed in the game. Believed in its virtues. In what it revealed of character. What it showed of a man. Merely thinking of those wonderful Hospital Cup victories made him straighten his back as he walked; they put an extra spring in his step, the air was fresh in his lungs, that's more like it, not breathless at all, just a slight twinge in his right knee, old cartilage damage, nothing serious, as the seventy-year-old cantered up to the rose garden for the second time and romped home.

Before tea he would go on up and see the old boy. He would go upstairs, hoping to elude Clementine and Colville, and check how Winston was coming along: see if his eyes had unclouded, see if he was less grey about the gills, see if his words had untangled, check the strength in his grip, if possible do some routine tests with the ophthalmoscope, have a quiet chat with the nurse. She might have spotted something one way or the other.

The next forty-eight hours were critical.

He might make it, he might not.

Things sometimes just come to an end.

No, come on, Charles!

Hope springs. Hope springs eternal.

But the old boy had never been like this before.

Would be terrible if he were left not dead but disfigured.

Near miss or dead cert, life or death.

Could boil down not to medicine or will power but to luck.

Pot luck.

Like a bullet in the trenches. Like a shell. Or a capsize.

Wouldn't it be good, though, to hear the old boy's tricks and mannerisms of speech again, to see him back on top form, dwarfing the others around him by the sheer force of his personality . . . and looking for a scrap, any sort of scrap, even the sort of thing Charles started to remember, starting to smile as he did so:

'Charles, did I ever tell you, when I was young a black depression settled on me, and the light faded from my life? Did I tell you that? And I don't like standing near the edge of a railway platform. When an express train roars past I like a pillar between me and the train. Did I ever tell you that?'

'Yes, you did.'

'Did I?'

'Yes.'

'You don't seem very concerned. As my doctor.'

'You haven't done too badly, all things considered, for a man with a black depression in a fading light.'

'Be that as it may, Charles, we've got to do something about the bloody Russians. Charles? What do you suggest? Charles, I asked you a question.'

'Your territory, I think.'

'Oh, for God's sake,' Winston shouted, slamming down his drink, 'why do I bother to talk to you! You're not interested in my health, and you're not interested in Russia!'

'Don't shout at me. You're behaving badly.'

'I am?'

'You are.'

'You wouldn't prefer to look after Mr Attlee, then? Take him on instead of me?'

Moran exploded.

'What did you just say to me? What did you just say!'

'Only joking.'

'Would you prefer another doctor? Because if so that is increasingly attractive to me.'

'In view of your salvo, Charles, all troops surrender immediately. Hoist yellow flag.'

Smiling at the memories, and thankful for the quips, Moran nodded to the detective outside the back door. After two circuits of the gardens the doctor had, as he knew he would, recovered his equilibrium. In the future he would try to be more civil to Colville. He would unbend a bit. He wiped his feet on the mat, and he entered the house to the welcoming smell of fresh scones from the kitchen.

*

The next night, alone in her own bedroom, Clementine resumed her talk to her husband. She had intended to do this sitting by his bed, and had gone there again to do so, and had very quietly opened the door only to come across a startled Nurse Appleyard rubbing his feet.

At first Clementine was not at all sure what on earth was going on. She thought she must be mistaken, she had never seen the like, she was shocked, but that was indeed the case. Massaging. While her husband lay there, oblivious to the world around him, Nurse Appleyard had uncovered his legs from his calves down, placed them on a large white towel, and was slowly rubbing cream of some sort into the soles of his feet, his ankles and his toes.

If it wasn't one thing it was another. If Nurse Appleyard wasn't holding Winston's hand it seemed she was now rubbing cream into his feet, with a glimpse of his bare white bottom! Clementine found it oddly disturbing and intrusive to witness and turned on her heel.

*

'And there's something I haven't told you. To be honest, Winston, I was sworn to secrecy about it. So far only Jock Colville and I have been let in on it. It was meant to be a lovely surprise for you. But who cares about silly secrets now? From what I have just seen in your bedroom there aren't any left.

'Next year, when you're eighty, both Houses want to give you a portrait. As an eightieth birthday present. Yes, a portrait of you, isn't that lovely, by whom hasn't yet been decided, anyway a portrait of you by whichever artist they choose, to hang in the Palace of Westminster. The greatest of honours for the greatest parliamentarian, the greatest war leader and the greatest of men. That is how it was put to me, and that is a description of you, my darling.

'I know only too well how you'd like to look in your portrait. You'd like to be in your finest robes, in all your finery, wouldn't you? The Order of the Garter, the highest order, the pinnacle of chivalry. You do like dressing up, and what better way than in the image and the arms of St George? "Portrait of the Prime Minister dressed in the Order of the Garter". *Honi soit qui mal y pense.* And the Order of the Garter would give the picture a splash of colour, wouldn't it, and keep any suggestion of the black dog away. And we all know how much you do love strong colour in paintings.

'Well, my dear, how will you look *now* when you're hanging on the wall? Will it be "Portrait of old bulldog in black coat, stricken but still barking"? You've never liked losing face, have you, so God help us if the commission goes to one of the modern art lot, with their eye for the crippled and their love of the grotesque, they'll have an absolute field day. Imagine that Francis Bacon chap being let loose on you tonight!

'I thought you would die of grief after the Dardanelles. But you didn't. And even in the darkest days of 1940, when we were sleeping in the stale air of the underground war rooms, I never felt as bad as I do now. You were awake most of most nights, in the map room or on the telephone to President Roosevelt, or dealing with the generals, but I always felt we were going forward, never going back.

'Even when you were in the trenches with the Royal Scots Fusiliers, yes even then. We were young of course, and of course I was terrified. But not hopeless. Never hopeless. With death all around you day and night I still believed you would come back to me. To us. But I'll tell you what, a bit of foot massage from Nurse Appleyard won't bring you back from this, not to your full strength.'

Oh, dear God, please bring him back to me.

Please.

'And if you do come back?

'It's . . . unjustifiable to continue. It really is, Winston. In the name of heaven it's best for you to accept your limits and to resign. It's best for us both, best for you to go, best for all, best for the country. It's right and proper and long past time. You're no longer sitting on some Olympian platform above the rest of the world. You have to come down to earth and be treated like other men. Leave before the sponge is drawn across the slate. That's one of your phrases, isn't it? And it would be . . . kind to me. I know you don't want to be a bystander, don't want to put your feet up, you'd prefer the bayonet, I know that. But you can write more and you do write so well.

'You know I don't like Chartwell, I never did. You bought it without telling me. You brought the children down here behind my back and told them you were buying it, but kept me in the dark. That was unkind of you. Well, here we are. In your Chartwell. And I will try to be happy here if you will try to be sensible, if you try not to be outlandish. I don't like the Riviera either, even less the people. But we'll go there and we can spend more time in Cap Ferrat or Monte Carlo and you can paint, you can go off and paint all day, paint, paint, paint to your heart's content. So I'm not suggesting deckchairs at dawn, I can't see you doing the crossword, it will be more fun than that. You can even go, if go you must, to your ghastly casino. And late at night, when you've left the tables and collected your winnings or accepted your losses, when you come back home, to please me, just to please me, could we play some hands of bezique? I love bezique.

'Is that too much for a wife to ask? For me to ask? Is it? After all these years?'

*

Two very different sounds.

Honking geese and a soft rustle.

First the geese were there, then there was a pause, then he opened his eyes to that rustle.

He thought he knew the geese. Yes. Listen. Yes, of course. He'd know them anywhere. They would be flying over the garden, over the lakes most probably, taking their time to beat their wings and taking their time to squawk.

The soft rustling sound, a feminine sound, he did not at first recognise. Straining to listen again, he thought it might be a page being turned. A page being slowly and carefully turned. Perhaps he had imagined it. Perhaps he was dreaming. A minute or so passed. He wasn't properly awake and he had all but lost interest in whatever the sound was when it happened again, and clearly coming from the window.

And there, in the frame, was a woman's outline, and within a few seconds her outline started to fill out and become a person.

Who was this?

It wasn't Clementine.

He did not know who she was. A uniform.

She must be a nurse.

He watched her standing there, then moving, and he noticed the way she moved. She moved … gracefully. That was the word. She was absorbed in a book, unconsciously taking little steps to left or right with her eyes held on the page. Then she did something extraordinary: she smelt the book. He was sure that is what she did. She slowly inhaled it.

'Nurse?'

Nurse Appleyard had rarely felt such a shock. She hurriedly put the book down as if caught red-handed.

'Yes, sir?'

'Nurse? Could you—'

'Yes, sir. I'm here.'

Her first instinct was to rush out of the bedroom and shout from the top of the stairs, 'He's talking! Doctor, Lady Churchill, Mr Colville, come *now*, he's talking!' Instead, she managed to control herself. She told herself she was a good nurse and must hold her nerve and maintain her composure. This was the last moment to be doing something dramatic like running out. Calmness was needed. She must behave as if this was the most normal of nurse and patient exchanges. She came to his bedside, looking down on him. And she smiled. A most lovely smile.

'Nurse? I wondered—'

'Let's just tuck that pillow in there, shall we … A little bit of support will help.'

'What day is it?'

'Thursday.'

He stared at her. Thursday? No.

'Thursday?'

'Yes, and the sun is shining.'

She must keep him talking. The doctor was very clear about that.

'How long was I asleep?'

'Oh, I'm not really sure, quite a while anyhow. You obviously needed it. Nothing better than a good sleep. That's what I always say. I love a good sleep, don't you?'

He looked at her as she straightened his bed.

'What is your name?'

'I'm Nurse Appleyard and I've come to look after you.'

'Apples?'

He seemed to struggle for a moment. Then he tried again.

'May I ask you your . . . Christian name?'

She leant across him.

'It's Millie.'

'Millie?'

'Yes.'

'And may I call you Millie?'

'If you like, sir. Or nurse. I don't mind.'

Had he seen her before? Might have done. He was not sure. Never mind, he was glad she was with him. There was no busy-ness in her movements, he liked that, and above all she didn't bustle. She seemed to glide around the bed. Yes, glide.

'You were reading.'

'I shouldn't have been, the doctor would be very angry.'

'Reading ... is a wonderful thing.'

'I couldn't live without it.'

'I am so glad that ... you were reading.'

To start with his words came in a measured way, as if he was searching for them and there was a time delay, then they became stronger. It was as if he had been somewhere else, resting, or as if he had regressed for a while, that was all, and was now ready to return to the stage.

'I took one of your books off your shelf. I thought you were asleep.'

'I was asleep. I think we can all agree on that. And I feel I may well be going to ... nod off again.'

'That's all right. Why not?'

His eyelids flickered.

'I like turtle soup.'

'I don't think I've ever had it.'

There was a very fetching way she held her head a little to one side as she spoke, as if she were assessing him as well as still apologising for the book, not that there was any need to. She had smelt the book. He was sure he saw that. And another thing, he liked her voice. If there was one thing he could never abide, apart from a loudly ticking clock, it was a woman with a high-pitched voice. Clementine, Clemmie, had the most beautiful voice, everyone said so. Oh, the importance of the voice. *Her voice was ever soft, gentle and low, an excellent thing in woman.*

He was gone.

*

She was there with him again.

'Where did that come from, nurse? And who said it?'

He was back with her.

'Where does what come from, sir?'

It was Shakespeare.

'It's Shakespeare. *Her voice was ever soft.*'

'I'm sorry, sir, I didn't catch that. Did I hear you say Shakespeare?'

His eyes hurt.

Little bright lights and grey dots raced and swam in them.

Shakespeare, one of his plays, somewhere.

But which? And where?

His forehead did not feel quite right.

Nor did his fingers. They felt fat.

It was all so . . . aggravating.

A to Z.

So, start with A.

Yes, start with the As. See if your memory is still . . .

Antony, without an h.

Anthony, as in Anthony Eden, has an h.

'There's no h in the play *Antony and Cleopatra.*'

'Is that so, sir?'

Antony and Cleopatra.

No, *All's Well That Ends Well* comes before that.

That shows the . . . grey cells are still there.

Then comes *Antony and Cleopatra.*

Without an h.

As You Like It is next. Alphabetically speaking.

But, no, he could not for the life of him remember who said *Her voice was ever soft, gentle and low, an excellent thing in woman.* Nor who it was said of. Of whom it was said. His head was now foggy and beginning to throb. Bs. Any Bs? Cs were easy. *Coriolanus. Cymbeline.* But not the Bs. Before he had decided if there were any Bs, did he hear himself say, or was it Nurse Appleyard who heard him say,

'Bomb. A bomb has been.'

'It's all right, sir.'

'We have spilt the atom. Not spilt. Not spilt. *Split* the atom. I have just heard. A bomb. A big bomb. When the future opens its jaws it's hard to look back.'

Nurse Appleyard stroked his hand. He seemed to like that. The furrows slowly left his face. And she thought she felt him squeeze her hand back. Yes, there, he did it again. His eyelids were heavy, heavier, so heavy, and even before his wife and the doctor could hurry in he had slipped away.

*

'Winston is back'.

That was the signal sent by the Admiralty to the Fleet on the outbreak of war in September 1939. Well, Winston was back, back with them now in Chartwell, albeit up and down, albeit fitful and untuned, but restored. They had all seen him,. Lady Churchill, Lord Moran and Jock Colville, and all had spoken to him. Rab Butler sent a message. The children drove down at different times and sat, smiling, at his bedside. They met Nurse Appleyard and heard her account of his return and told her how grateful they were for all she had done.

Though very tired and variable in mood, the Prime Minister was less pallid and more alert. His recall was a bit hit and miss, but, generally speaking, as the days passed he was hitting more than he was missing. His arms were moving better. There was a little more response in his feet. Ridiculously, characteristically, he even announced he wanted to go for a walk. They squashed that one pretty quickly.

Overall, though no one was being over-confident, he was on the right road.

And over supper with Lord Moran and Jock Colville – a warm summery evening with not a breath of air in the Weald – Clementine told her favourite stories of Winston.

How Winston had never been on a bus. How Winston had only once been on an underground train and that was in the General Strike when Clementine deposited him at South Kensington and he went round and round the Circle Line not knowing how or where to get off. He had to be rescued and stumbled up and out into the street hot and gasping for air.

'Marvellous,' Jock said.

Heard that one a million times, Moran said to himself.

'And you remember his reaction to the film of *Wuthering Heights*? As we were coming out of the cinema someone asked Winston what he thought of it and he said, "Terrible weather they have in Yorkshire."'

'Priceless,' Colville said.

Heard that one as well.

'And then there was Sawyers and the hot water bottle,' Clementine went on.

Oh yes, the valet and the lost hot water bottle.

'Delicious asparagus, by the way,' Jock said.

'But you must have heard the hot water bottle one before, surely!'

'No, I don't think so,' Jock said.

'No, never,' Moran managed.

'Well, he'd lost his hot water bottle, and couldn't find it, and you know what Winston is like when he can't find something, talk about a bear with a sore head, anyway he became very exercised and he demanded Sawyers find out where it was. "You're sitting on it, sir," poor old Sawyers said, "not a very good idea." "It's not an idea," Winston said, "it's a coincidence."'

'*Typique*,' Jock said.

Moran put down his fork and brought up Winston and poetry.

'Poetry?'

'That's what he said he wanted. When I was with him just now.'

'Poetry?'

'Couldn't have been clearer. Poetry.'

Clementine leapt at it:

'Oh yes, I see what you mean, he *loves* poetry. What a good idea, Charles! He loves listening to poetry, loves being read to, loves reciting it out loud. We can take it in turns. He'll be in his element.'

'Much better than reciting Russian names,' Colville said.

'What do you mean?'

'That's what he was doing this morning when I went up, I presume to show me he could remember them. Molotov, Malenkov, Kuznetsov, Kalinin, Zhukov.'

'He's obsessed with Russia,' Clementine said.

'He was bordering on the unstoppable. Then he started to quiz me over why the butterflies weren't as numerous as usual.'

'Oh, take no notice,' Clementine said, 'he says that every year.'

'Poetry can't do much harm, I suppose,' Moran said.

'So,' Colville said, wincing at the last remark, '*The Oxford Book of Verse* it is. Plenty to dip into there.'

'*English* verse,' Clementine said.

'Absolutely, nothing foreign,' Colville agreed.

'We don't want him becoming any more anti-frog,' Moran said.

Colville glared and, turning away from Moran, settled into a private exchange with Clementine.

'Tennyson's the way forward.'

'Plus a bit of Byron perhaps.'

'Or Browning at a pinch, but nothing too modern.'

'No Mr Eliot then?'

'No, Winston gives him a wide berth.'

'Longfellow's more his line.'

'Oh, he absolutely sails through his Longfellow.'

'*And* he can quote him,' Clementine said, rolling her eyes. 'At length.'

'Indeed,' Colville laughed.

'Why not suggest a few new ones for him to learn?' Moran said.

'Learn?' Colville asked.

'New ones? Why?' Clementine said.

'Good for his memory, mental exercise, gives him a target to aim at.'

'Possibly,' Colville said. 'It is true he loves a target.'

'You won a prize for verse at Harrow, didn't you, Jock?'

Colville smiled and turned back to Moran.

'Yes, Latin verse, that's right. In 1932. But how extraordinary! How on earth did you know that, Charles? Who let that one slip?'

'You did.'

*

She was sitting not to one side of him, as she often did, but in full view at the end of the bed. She was looking straight at him, scanning his face for any more signs, scrutinising the most famous face in the world as it rested right there on the pillow. His eyes were puffed up, his skin stretched smooth, and she was listening to his intermittent breathing or to a strange intestinal rumble. He was having one of his less good days. There were ups and there were sporadic lulls. The doctor said that was only to be expected.

Once or twice during the last week, fearing a relapse, fearing the worst, she had found her heart starting to race and her chest to thump in a flurry of panic and she started to think, what happens if. What Happens If. But her anxiety soon passed. The Prime Minister, it was clear, was far from finished.

'Ah, Millie . . . You're still there.'

'And keeping a close eye on you.'

'I was dreaming I was dead.'

'Were you?'

'And my body was under a white sheet in an empty room. My bare feet were sticking out from under the sheet. It was very lifelike. Though I was dead of course.'

'Well, the good thing is you're not.'

He smiled his seraphic smile.

'I lie here, you know, and things come racing back. If they ever happened.'

'What things?'

'That's the point. I feel lost half way up a ladder. Should I go up or down?'

Diverting his incoherence, pretending she had not heard, she tucked a large napkin round his neck, dabbing both sides of his mouth as she did so.

'Better pop that napkin there . . . keep things nice and tidy. There, that's it.'

'And you've fed the goldfish?'

'I did. Lovely colours, aren't they? And more of them than I expected.'

She started, as unobtrusively as possible, to tidy his disordered bed. His body was slightly skewed and she helped him to lie a little straighter.

'Is the cat there?'

'Sorry, sir?'

'Did you count them, the goldfish?'

'Should I have done?'

'If Marmaduke's on the windowsill, always count the goldfish. Little beauties, aren't they?'

'They are, yes.'

'I'd make love to them, if I only knew how.'

'You're naughty, Prime Minister.'

'Am I saucy, or am I daft? Millie-Molly?'

She laughed.

'Which is it . . . ? I've forgotten your name again. Was I close?'

'It's Millie. And it doesn't matter.'

'Oh, it does. I would not like to be called Willy or Wally. I do not feel I am a Willy Churchill or a Wally Churchill. My deepest apology. Names go, you know, as you get older. Things . . . silt up.'

'Never mind if they do.'

She looked so fresh-faced to him and so young.

'Tell me . . . I lie here and things . . . places . . . Omdurman, Ploegsteert . . . no, I've said that. No, I haven't. Tell me, when you were a little girl, did you jump puddles? My daughters did. Sarah did. And Diana did. And Mari-gold. No, she was not old enough to—'

He put a hand over his eyes and sniffed and gulped. Then loudly blew his nose. Nurse Appleyard busied herself with something.

'What was it like for you, Millie, growing up? Were the hedgerows and the ditches full of cow parsley?'

'I probably didn't notice.'

'But did you hop and skip all the way home from school?'

'Part of the way. It was three miles to school. Just under.'

'Millie?'

'Yes?'

'May I have a drink?'

'Of course.'

She poured him some water.

'A large brandy tends to keep me going.'

'Now you know that is not allowed. Doctor's orders. You know I can't.'

'A port then. Port is not a real drink. I'll tell you where it is.'

She was trying not to smile.

'It's water or lemon.'

He petulantly slapped the bedclothes.

'And I'd pinned my hopes on you! I thought we were getting on so well and you would see my point of view. Or at the very least you would lace my tea with a little something. No? There's not much fun left, is there? I am . . . stranded . . . I am empty-handed. Is this a life? Clinging on. Languishing. Blown every which way. It gets my goat.'

'You need to be patient.'

'Well, I don't care.'

'Well, we all care about you. Very much. The whole country does.'

No sooner was the sharp anger there in his eyes than it had dissolved itself.

'Do you think so? The *whole* country, I am not sure about that.'

Tears were rolling down his smooth, plump cheeks. He was unable to check them, and made no effort to do so.

'I blub an awful lot, you know. It always catches me unawares. You'll have to get used to it.'

'I don't mind, I don't mind at all.'

'School songs at Harrow. That's when I blub the most. I must ask Jock Colville if he does. We were at the same school, you know.'

'Why shouldn't we cry? I know I do.'

'Do you?'

'Yes, when I think of my rabbit buried up there in Yorkshire.'

'What was your rabbit's name?'

'Flopsy. We all love Beatrix Potter at home.'

'Flopsy,' he said.

'Mopsy,' she said.

'Cotton-tail.'

'And Pe-ter!'

He grasped her arm with his outstretched fingers.

'Don't leave me, will you?'

'No, I won't leave you.'

'Don't be long.'

'I just said ... I'm not leaving. I am not going anywhere.'

'I'm worried they might replace you with a head-scarfed housewife, and I'll wake up to find Maggie Mutton dressed up as lamb. Sorry. What am I talking about now?'

'There are many better nurses than me, sir.'

'No, you're wrong. But because I enjoy our chats ... Let me show you something.'

He slowly rolled up the right sleeve of his pyjamas, the veins branching up his arm, his skin china white.

'Can you see?'

She looked at the inside of his right arm, just below the elbow.

'It's a scar, isn't it? It's very faint.'

'That's over fifty years ago.'

'What happened?'

'A skin graft. After the Battle of Omdurman in 18 ... 98, yes 1898, I gave some of my skin to a friend. To a dear friend. He was injured. In the charge of the Twenty-first Lancers. It hurt like hell having the skin taken off, I can tell you.'

'I'm sure it did.'

'I gave it to Dick Molyneux. He died a few weeks ago. Jock told me that yesterday, or the day before. Or I think he did. Yes, he did. Dick's a goner. It seems that Sir Richard Molyneux has taken my skin on ahead with him. As an advance guard into the next world.'

'That's a funny way of putting it.'

But he was into his stride and playing to the gallery.

'This hand, this hand, you see it, Millie, this hand held a sabre at the Battle of Omdurman. I was on horseback, with a sabre, charging the enemy. Can you see me waving a sabre? On a cavalry charge? In 18 ... in 1898? That's a long time ago, 1898, when I was with Kitchener in the Sudan. A full forty years or so after the Charge of the

Light Brigade. Different battle. That was at the Battle of Balaclava in 185 . . .4. Yes, 1854. Or have I said that?'

'No, you've never mentioned any of this.'

'Anyway, I cannot complain. I don't think things are too bad, do you, if I can remember a name like Dick Molyneux?'

Suddenly he'd had enough of all this talk of cavalry charges, the energy drained from him and he fell slowly back, with a quiet, exhausted sigh. She straightened his sheet, watching his eyes close. He soon settled to slower breathing, so it was a surprise to her when he spoke:

'And I'll tell you what, Millie.'

'What's that?'

'There'll be a bloody row if I recover.'

A small, determined smile passed over his face as, sabre in hand, he mounted his charger and faced the foe.

When can their glory fade?
O the wild charge they made!
All the world wondered.
Honour the charge they made,
Honour The Light Brigade,
Noble six hundred.

*

As far as Jock Colville was concerned, what had been proving an agreeably amusing, indeed almost a celebratory dinner was (he confided later in his diary) utterly ruined, and not for the first time, by two ham-fisted remarks from Moron, the muddied oaf. From the bull in the china shop with, if you will allow the conflation, a chip on both shoulders.

Not only was the Moron's anti-frog remark completely uncalled for in front of Clementine, he then chose to be deliberately and gratuitously offensive about the Macaulay-Haughton prize for Latin verse he had won two years running as a boy at Harrow.

Furthermore, it was only a short while ago, at a moment when the morale of the household was most delicately poised, that the man had barged in unannounced and been unspeakably rude, berating him over the tricky press bulletin on Winston's health, as if the Prime Minister's private secretary could over-rule the Chancellor of the Exchequer. He seemed to have not a shred of an idea about the nature of governance or the art of the possible.

Even given that Winston's judgement of 'his people' had never been his strongest suit, it was a mystery what on earth he ever saw in the first place, let alone still continued to see in his doctor. As for Clementine, it was an open secret that she couldn't stand him.

The man was a black cloud. The man was a congenital grouser. Worse, he had no breeding, no manners, no tact and no sense of his own limitations. For example, the fact that he was woefully ill-read was self-evident. He was a medic after all, and one could more or less live with a lack of culture as long as the uncultured knew when to shut up. What one could not and would not tolerate, however, was his prickly pushiness. He was pushy in the very worst kind of way, push, push, push, and painfully unaware when he was socially and intellectually out of his depth.

Pushy and prickly and inept.

What a triumvirate.

Oh, and northern. Or From The North, as those from the north could never stop reminding you. As if you couldn't tell. What was it about people from that particular county, why did they keep saying 'I'm from Yorkshire' or, worse, 'I'm Yorkshire'? Did people go around the place saying 'I'm Hertfordshire' or 'I'm Herefordshire' or 'I'm Hampshire'? No, they did not.

Things had reached a new and farcical low just before the Prime Minister's stroke when, to acute embarrassment all round in Number 10, he asked Winston if he would put in a good word for him as the next Provost of Eton. Good God. Imagine, just imagine would you for a moment, the Moron as the Provost of Eton!

It made one shudder. It made one laugh. Even an Old Harrovian wouldn't wish that one on Eton.

And he had an infinite capacity for misreading the signals. Be generous and invite the Moron to luncheon and he settled in for the week-end. It was as bad as asking someone how they were and then having to listen to them telling you. He was always staying when he should leave, always speaking when he should be silent and, worst of all, always assuming he was part of the family when he wasn't.

Yes, of course, he was loyal to Winston, but it was the loyalty of the leech.

*

After Lady Churchill had left, she took his wrist.

'First your pulse, then a quick check on the blood pressure.'

'Now?'

'Doctor's orders. You heard him tell me.'

'And then my feet?'

'If you're good.'

Two of her fingers rested on his vein. She pressed his skin lightly with an eye on the second hand of her watch. They were silent, aware of the minute's intimacy. In the distance a lawn was being mown. She smiled and took her hand away.

'That's fine,' she said. 'Good and regular.'

'Am I normal?'

'That is a very big question, sir.'

He laughed.

'So you like reading?'

'I do, sir.'

'So do I.'

'Very much.'

'So do I, Molly.'

'It's Millie. And not Molly and not Mandy.'

'Millie. Millie! Of course it is. And have you ever read *Treasure Island*?'

'I have, yes. Everyone has, I'm sure of that.'

'And what is the first thing you think of if I say *Treasure Island*?'

Nurse Appleyard's eyes started to smile as she said, 'Oh, that's easy. Jim Hawkins and the apple barrel.'

'Yes! Jim Hawkins and the apple barrel! We agree!'

'It was read out loud to us at school, Mr Hayes it was, our teacher at our school in Bradford, in Yorkshire, and he said before he started that it was a bit of a boys' book but he hoped we girls would like it. Like it? I loved it. He read a chapter to us all at the end of the day.'

'Before you ran off home?'

'Before we ran home, yes.'

'And what, may I ask, was your view of Long John Silver?'

The smile faded a little from her face.

'My view?'

'Yes.'

'I don't know. I mean, my view doesn't really matter, does it?'

'It does to me, Millie. It matters a great deal. And as we seem to be agreeing on most things, how does he strike you?'

'Am I back in school now, sir?'

'Back in school?'

'Because that is how I am feeling.'

'Am I behaving like a tyrant?'

His jaw was set.

'No, you're not. It's just that I—'

'Because my wife sometimes says I do. She reminded me a few moments ago of my tyranny. That I behave like one. A tyrant.'

'I wouldn't know about that, sir.'

'So you won't even tell me if you like Long John?'

'I'm not sure whether I like him or not.'

'Please go on, Millie.'

She started to move around the room a little as she talked.

'Well, he's bad, he's wicked, he's a villain, isn't he, but he sweeps you off your feet, if you know what I mean. And you can't get him out of your mind, and I can see him now.'

'"I can see him now." What greater compliment could an author ask from his reader than "I can see him now"?'

'With his one leg.'

'And his parrot on his shoulder.'

'Pieces of eight!'

'Pieces of eight!'

They both laughed. The Prime Minister cackled on until he started to cough, a long eye-bulging episode which subsided into a spell of breathless wheezing.

'Take a sip. Please. That should help.'

He sipped the water, his hand trembling a little, his tone suddenly pugnacious.

'You mustn't fuss me. It's not good for me. Because I need to get back on my pins. By next week I will be walking. You will tell them I'm getting better, won't you?'

Avoiding his gaze and his question, she took back the tumbler.

'They want me to retire, Millie. Oh, yes, they do.'

'Do they?'

'And did you know that Long John was based on a real man? On one of Stevenson's best friends.'

'No.'

'Well, he was.'

'Can you do that? Is that allowed for a writer?'

'Well, they do.'

'You mean Stevenson didn't make it all up?'

'No. He used his best friend as a model. A model villain.'

'He shouldn't have, that's not right.'

'You feel that strongly?'

'Yes, that's disloyal, that is. I'd never do that to a friend.'

'Oh, writers do that sort of thing all the time. They're a most shocking bunch. They'd kill their grannies for a few sales. They don't care a fig about morals.'

It was on the tip of Millie's tongue to say, But you're a writer, sir, you're a famous writer, but she didn't. Instead she said,

'But they're educated.'

'That's true.'

'And they should know better.'

'Being educated doesn't stop you doing bad things. Nor is being clever everything. A long life in politics has made that very clear to me. The appalling Heydrich, the very worst of the *Nar-zees*, was very educated. He loved playing his Schubert. Let me show you something.'

Churchill pointed to the big bookcase to the left of his bedroom window.

'Would you get a book for me? Please. Second row from the top.'

She walked across and reached up.

'No, second I said, that's the third. About ten or fifteen books in, I think, from the left. I can't quite see it from here. It has a blue cover.'

She was now up on tiptoe and moving from left to right like a ballet dancer on her points.

'The spine may be a little torn. Henley. The poems of W.E. Henley. That's what you're looking for. A blue book, faded blue. That's what I call my snob bookcase, it's where I keep all my best books. Well, no, more my particular favourites. Any luck?'

'Never seen so many books. There are books everywhere, all over the house. As for your study next door!'

She eased the green book out of a tightly packed shelf, turned and held it up.

'This one?'

'That's it. Well done.'

'It's green.'

'It may look green to you, but it's blue. Would you bring it over, please? Thank you. You have exceedingly pretty hands.'

'No, I don't.'

'Yes, you do, I've noticed them many times.'

'I don't know what to say when people say nice things to me. Not that they do. Much.'

'You could start with thank you. Let's start again. You have exceedingly pretty hands.'

'Thank you. Henley. What is special about his poems?'

'Oh, they have given me great solace over the years.'

'I've never even heard of him.'

'Well, Henley was the inspiration for Long John Silver. There's no doubt about that at all.'

'Did he only have one leg then?'

'Exactly! Spot on, Millie.'

'And a parrot on his shoulder?'

'No, sadly, there was no parrot on his shoulder. As far as I know.'

'Oh, pity.'

'And I'll tell you something, between these four walls: for many years I had a bird that liked to sit on my shoulder.'

'Now you're laughing at me.'

'I'm not. I had a green budgerigar, Toby, sadly no longer with us, who liked to sit on my shoulder or my head. Or on my spectacles. And even, the little devil, he would sometimes alight on the rim of my glass. He also, for his sins, had been known to sip my whisky and soda.'

'Really?'

'It's true. Anyway, in 1874, in the very year I was born, I was born in Blenheim, yes, in 1874, Henley went up to Edinburgh, to the Infirmary, because it looked as if he would lose his other leg. He was twenty-five. One leg had been taken off when he was a young boy and now a second amputation seemed certain.'

'That's terrible.'

'That's how the cards fell for him. We have little say,

Millie, in how our hand is dealt. But Henley did not lie down under his burden. He had heard there was a great doctor up there in Edinburgh, a great pioneering surgeon, Joseph Lister. And great men can change the world.'

'I know that.'

She knew she was talking to one.

'So Henley got himself up from Gloucester to Edinburgh and while he was a patient in the Infirmary, and he was a patient a long time, he was visited by Robert Louis Stevenson, who knew of Henley's poetry. Stevenson had also heard of Henley's larger than life character, his huge personality, and wanted to meet him. And they became firm friends.'

Churchill pointed to the chair next to his bed.

'Could you linger for a moment longer? And then we can go on talking.'

'I'll be here as long as you like, sir.'

'Right. The very first poem in the book. What's it called?'

'"Enter Patient".'

'No, got that wrong, the second or third poem, then. "The Operation"?'

'Yes, here it is.'

'Read it out loud to me. I love listening to poetry. If I can't smoke and I can't drink and I can't assault a canvas at least I can lie here and listen to a poem. I am in your hands. Your exceedingly pretty hands.'

Nurse Appleyard stood up in open alarm, her eyes scanning the lines.

'No, no, sir, I can't. We've all heard you on the wireless. I couldn't read to you.'

'Yes, you can.'

'No, not to you, sir. I'm just a nurse.'

'*Just a nurse!* That won't do. That's not you talking. You're not like that. It won't do at all, you know, to talk in that way. Never say that again! Where would this country be without nurses? More to the point, where would I be at this very moment?'

'The thing is, I'm not good with words.'

'Yes, you are, you're very good with words.'

'And it's too sad for me, this poem. There's enough sadness in the world already.'

'It's not sad, it is true. It is what Henley found. And, as a nurse, you will see how far we have come in eighty years. In medicine.'

She was partly looking at him, partly at the poem.

'I know, it is wonderful what doctors can do now. I've stood next to them and seen it.'

'All you need to do is imagine you are back in 1874. Imagine you are a man, it's good to put yourself in the shoes of the opposite sex. Go further, imagine you are a one-legged man with a crutch, don't laugh, you've got yourself up to Edinburgh, long journey, and you have walked up a cobbled Edinburgh street, walking painfully, tap tap tap goes your crutch, and then you go up the steps into an imposing, high building. Can you see it?'

'Very clearly.'

'It could even be a jail. You are admitted. You are

frightened, who would not be? But you are in the hands of a great surgeon.'

She breathed out slowly, as if growing in resolve.

'Can I read it to myself a few times? Can I practise?'

'But you must. That's what I always do before I speak in public.'

'You're teasing me.'

'I wouldn't do that, would I?'

'Oh, I think you would.'

She swallowed and straightened her skirt.

'I wish you hadn't asked me to do this.'

'Millie. Mill-*ie*.'

'Sir?'

'The Prime Minister, the old so-and-so, orders you to read "The Operation". No, as a favour, the Prime Minister begs you, cap in hand, to read the poem. Take your time. Poetry is much better, in my considered opinion, if it is spoken slowly.'

'Don't you worry, sir, I'll be slow.'

'Because the slower the better. It helps the listener to absorb the words, and to savour the thoughts, and to feel the emotion. Never hurry. Take your time, because if they're given time to work words come alive and stay in the mind. President Truman used to speak one hundred and forty words a minute. It's too fast. Too fast. Gabble, gabble, gabble, that was the President. Never hurry. Never.'

'What happened to Henley? Did he lose his other leg?'

'No, thanks to the consummate skill of his surgeon he did not. But, on poetry, remember the simplicity of the words and the depth of the feeling. That is what stirs our hearts. But I'd like to sit up for it. For your performance.'

'Give me your arm, then. Put your arm on my shoulder. You're going to help me here. Now lift, that's it, that's very good. There.'

Once he was settled and sitting up, she stepped back. He was beaming at her.

'I will soon be out of bed and walking.'

She looked down at the poems in her hands.

Her own heart was beating hard. She was amazed she was about to do such a thing, but he was so funny and so warm she would do anything for him, even though she could never tell anyone she'd done it, not a living soul, because she was sworn to secrecy, wasn't she. Maybe one day, one day, she would be lucky enough to meet the right man and be married and have children, children she could (many years from now) tell about this.

What would she say?

Once upon a time, children, a long time ago, I was asked to read some poems out loud to the Prime Minister, oh yes I was, as he lay very ill in his bed in Chartwell. And I like to think I helped him get better. What poems were they, Mum? Famous poems by Shakespeare, were they? *No, not at all, they weren't famous at all, but I'll tell you who was famous and that's the Prime Minister we had then, he was very famous indeed, one of the greatest men who ever lived, and in a minute I'll tell you something else, something about a man with one leg.*

*

Mensa, mensa, mensam . . .

It was one of his late night party routines, one of his best after-dinner turns, and a particular favourite with Jock Colville, but this time it was performed from his bed for only one man: Charles Moran. He was determined to prove to his doctor that his old grey cells were working. Not only was his body becoming much stronger, as he would soon show to be the case, but so was his mind.

'*Mensa. A* table. *Mensa! O* table! *Mensam. A* table. *Mensae. Of* a table. *Mensae. To or for* a table. *Mensa. By, with or from* a table. What on earth does it mean? Were you any good at Latin, Charles?'

'Passably.'

'I was not. I am naturally biased in favour of the young learning English.'

'Well, they do.'

'By and large. Most of them. And I approve of their learning poems by heart. Indeed, I would insist upon it. That is what I am doing myself, that is my prep at the moment. A poem a day keeps the doctor away. No, don't take it personally, Charles, because I have one for you. Everyone who comes to visit me is to read a poem. Please ensure that a large notice is pinned outside. *All ye who enter here* . . . That is the way forward. Poems are part of the cure.'

'Jock can do poems in Latin for you if you wish.'

'Heaven forbid! No, I would let only the cleverest pupils learn Latin. As an honour.'

'Ah, very generous.'

'And Greek as a treat.'

'An intriguing approach to education.'

'I shall put it to the Party Conference.'

'Will you?'

'Yes.'

There was a pause. Moran refused to pick up the Conference hint. Neither man spoke, until:

'But tell me everything, dear Charles.'

'About what?'

'What have I missed of late? Tell me all.'

'Well, we won the Abingdon by-election.'

'If we ever lose Abingdon, the world, at least the world as I know it, will be over.'

'A bit like St Mary's not winning the Hospital Cup, you mean?'

'If you say so.'

'And Jock has no doubt told you the latest about Anthony?'

'The latest?'

'Yes. Jock has surely brought you up to scratch?'

'He may have. There's murmuring, there always is, and there always will be some boneless wonder whispering about whether whatshisname will be taking over from whodyoumacallit.'

'I don't follow.'

'It's in his eyes. In Anthony's. That time-to-make-way thingumajig. Handing over the baton.'

'That might be difficult, as he's still in Boston. Jock told me that he told you.'

'I said *bat*-on not *Bos*-ton.'

'I know you did. But Anthony Eden is in Boston, still in Boston. We arranged it, if you remember, with Dr Cattell some months ago. We all discussed it together in Number Ten. Then Anthony flew over there to get it sorted out. And, while he was away, you insisted that you took on foreign affairs as well.'

'In Boston, is he?'

'He was in the New England Baptist Hospital. And now he's convalescing with some friends, still in Boston. He won't be home for a while. I'm sure you know all that. Clementine told you as well.'

'Did she?'

The Prime Minister stared hard ahead, lips pressed close. Was he playing at being a bit slow, was he playing one of his games?

'Anyway, he's pulled through, Winston, but I understand he's not out of the wood yet.'

'What wood?'

'He's not out of it yet, I said. Anthony.'

'In Boston? Yes, yes, Charles, I'm with you.'

Moran had had enough of all this. His shoes hit the floor hard as he paced the room.

'You're being deliberately vague.'

'He can't wait. Hungry eyes. When-do-I-take-over eyes. The old baton business.'

'You've just said all that.'

'He cannot wait. That is his problem.'

'All things considered, I'd say Anthony's been rather

good at waiting, wouldn't you? Must be eight years or so.'

'I don't believe Anthony can do it. No point bringing the wrong chap in, is there, and it's cowardly to run away. Always look into their eyes, Charles. But you know that, you're a good judge of men, you had to be, didn't you, with your job in the trenches, yes?'

'In the Great War I was looking after the health of a whole battalion. Now it's the health of one man. Not sure which is the more difficult.'

The Prime Minister ignored this.

'Rab Butler hasn't got hungry eyes. You've probably noticed that.'

'If you say so.'

'Keeps a straight bat but never scores any runs, Rab Butler. Occupies the crease. That's Rab. Smells the roses but never gets round to picking them.'

'Is that the case?'

'Macmillan? Not so easy to tell with Macmillan.'

'Really?'

'More, much more, going on behind those eyes. Easier to translate Livy than to read Mac's eyes.'

Moran came back to his bedside.

'Well, fun though this is, Winston, we can't chat all day. And I don't want you to tire yourself out. But before I go I'd like to have a look at your legs. And your arms. See how much the massage is helping. See how we're coming on in that area. But we'll need the nurse's help. Won't be a moment.'

Moran went to the door and called her in. In the blink of an eye Nurse Appleyard appeared as if she was already on the alert and knew exactly what was required.

'Give me your arm, sir,' she said to the Prime Minister. He took her hand and they moved together like a couple before a formal dance. 'Put your arm on my shoulder. That's it. Now roll a little towards me, would you? That's very good. You're going to have to help me a little bit more. Yes.'

'Thank you, nurse,' the doctor said. 'Well done.'

'Doing terribly well,' Sir Winston said.

'Yes, you are, sir,' she said.

'No, no,' the Prime Minister said, 'Macmillan is.'

'It's all right, nurse, we were talking of other matters.'

'Oh, I'm sorry.'

'He's got gallstones,' Moran went on. 'So his doctor tells me.'

The Prime Minister started to smile, then beam.

'Gallstones? Macmillan? *Gall*-stones? *Has* he?'

'Yes. In acute pain.'

The Prime Minister was delighted.

'Is he? Poor chap. Acute pain? Dear-oh-dear-oh-dear.'

Winston was looking much better by the second, but Moran was increasingly uncomfortable that Nurse Appleyard was now a party to all this.

'It's all right, nurse. That's all for the moment, thank you.'

As the door shut behind her, Moran asked:

'So, Winston, who's in charge of the clattering train?'

'I am, Charles.'

'You are?'

'Just look at the state of the alternatives. Eden. Butler. Macmillan.'

Moran said nothing.

'I shall do what is best for the country. Circumstances may convince me of my indispensability. They need my name, you know.'

Moran again said nothing.

'Did you hear me, Charles?'

'Now the other arm. Flex your fingers, would you? Again. Clench, unclench. Now grip my hand. Harder. That's better.'

'I told you I'm better. You just don't listen.'

*

Nurse Appleyard could hear him as she approached his door.

Onward, Christian soldiers
Marching as to war,
With the cross of Jesus
Going on before.
Like a mighty ar-ar-mee
Steels against the foe
De-de-de-de-de-de-de
See his ban-
-ner
sgo

On-ward Chris-ti-an so-ho-ho-ul-diers

His purple dressing gown lay over the back of a chair. He was sitting, on the side of his bed, feet dangling, staring at the wall and twisting the end of his sheet into a loose knot. His singing voice was an out of tune croak.

'Prime Minister, it's me.'

'What?'

'It's me. Millie.'

He looked round but seemed not to see her. Had he slipped back? Was today one step forward, two steps back?

'More bad news, Millie?'

'No, not at all. It's still raining though. And a bit dark.'

He shook his finger in a warning gesture.

'No, these are not dark days. No, these are sombre days. There are no dark waters of despair. The tunnel may be long but at the end there will be light.'

'Oh, I'm sure there will be, sir. Now let's get you—'

'Let the House nag. Let the *Mirror* mock.'

'Lean on me a little. If that makes it any easier.'

She took his weight.

'They said they would defeat us in three weeks. In three weeks their generals said they would wring our necks like a chicken. Some chicken! Some neck! The Hun will be defeated and we will win the war against that evil tyranny. As for the French, they're a disgrace.'

'Are they?'

'But with the help of President Roosevelt, and the help of our allies, our brave allies, I'm sure all in the end will be—'

'That's it, let me help with that leg, it's a bit slow this one today, isn't it, and . . . just lie back a little.'

As she eased him back he tried to lever himself up once more, resisting, pushing hard against her, suddenly petulant.

'But how can I wage war with antiquated weapons! I am going to America. In the morning. It bled the country white, you know.'

'What did?'

'The Great War. And now we're at it again. But I must get dressed, I must go to America. I can't do everything off my own bat.'

Should she call the doctor? Or see if it passed? If it didn't she would.

'Maybe not just yet, not for a little while, sir, because—'

'Don't in-ter-*rupt*! And I need to show you what I sent today to his Majesty, appointing Anthony to take my place, no, *recommending* Anthony rather, it's for his Majesty to appoint, not my place, though I may *recommend* Anthony as the next Prime Minister, Anthony is to take over if I go down, because the U-boats could get me, you know, just as likely as the Luftwaffe, air, water, they're all over the show. Where is that letter, it was on the side table there, only a moment ago! Get it!'

Nurse Appleyard looked round.

'There's no letter, I'm afraid.'

'Yes, there is!'

'Not on your side table, sir. Not that I can see at the moment.'

He was shouting.

'So where did the woman put it? Is it asking too bloody

much for a bloody woman to put a simple piece of paper where it can be found! Is it! Doesn't know her arse from her elbow. She can't type and she can't spell and she can't put a bloody piece of paper where it can be found. Find it. I can't fight the war single-handed. It was the same ... after Singapore.'

Nurse Appleyard held his hand. Then she put her arm round his shoulders.

'Was it?'

'So humiliating. Singapore. To the Japs of all people. The Japs! The biggest humiliation in our history. *And* Rommel is on the rampage, with his advancing Panzers. What is going wrong with our people?'

'Shh. Shh. Come on, that's it. And in a minute, when you're nice and ready, I've got a glass of water here, and I'd like you to take your pill.'

'My pill?'

He did not speak for a minute or two. He had punctured. The false energy, the resistance and the random lucidity had gone out of him. He wheezed and gulped and shook his head and turned away as if embarrassed by his state and his recent speech. His face was podgy and rumpled.

Millie glanced at the ceiling. There was a small crack in the plaster above his bed. And the curtains, she noticed them too, the way they had faded a bit from years of sunlight. She moved slightly away from him, sensing he'd like to be left to himself for a moment, to collect himself and settle a bit, while she looked down on the lawns.

What a place it was, it was stunning, even in the rain. She loved the way the land fell gradually away towards the swimming pool and the lake, and then rose again, undulating, lifting your eye so you could see the cows dotted in the fields. She counted eleven of them. And to the far right, away into the distance, lay the Weald of Kent.

The garden was sodden from the downpour. Some crows were cruising around the wood. A beech tree creaked near the bedroom window. She heard his voice behind her, quieter now.

'What is going on? Mmm? In the world out there?'

'It's been raining. I did tell you.'

'Puddles?'

'Plenty of them. It's easing off a bit, though.'

'Easing off, is it?'

'More of a drizzle now. Then, before we know it, you'll see the sun come out, and gardens always look their best, don't you think, always look fresher, just after rain? Especially your garden here.'

'There doesn't seem much air about. Is it a bit stuffy today?'

'A bit close, yes.'

She turned into the room to face him. He blinked slowly. She smiled back. And then he looked again at her. His facial expressions were becoming more recognisable as he focused on her: he was becoming more him.

'Was I talking rubbish? A few moments ago? King Lear after the storm? I fear I was. Perhaps the blood wasn't getting round the backstreets.'

'You're fine now. All over. That's going to happen sometimes.'

'Rome wasn't built in a day.'

'No, nor was Redhill.'

He smiled at her.

'The wall, Millie, the wall round the vegetable garden? You know the one?'

'Yes.'

'You know it, don't you, you know the one I mean?'

'Yes, I pass the vegetable garden every day.'

'I built it, that wall, with these hands. Ask the men. And I mixed the cement. I did! I'm a bit of a dab hand, I can tell you, with a trowel. I'm a member of the Bricklayers Union, a card-carrying member, and I pay my dues. Tell your father that. I can see you don't believe me.'

She laughed.

'No, I do believe you.'

'I know I'm muddled, wandering a bit, a bit at sea. Well, I did build the wall, brick by brick. Bang the dinner gong and tell the whole world. The lakes, the dam and the swimming pool. I built them too.'

'I'm sure you did.'

He stared at her, nodding slowly.

'Nurse.'

'Yes?'

'Millie?'

'Yes?'

'I have not enjoyed July.'

'Come August you'll be fine.'

'So you don't think I should be put out to grass?'

'I'm just a nurse, sir.'

'I thought we weren't going to say that.'

'But it's true.'

'No. You're . . . my right arm. My safe mooring. You're the tops. You're the Mona Lisa.'

His eyes were brimming as he half sang the Cole Porter phrases, and she felt her own eyes prickle.

'Am I? If so I'm glad. Because you may need a right arm for a while and if you do find you want my right arm I'm here.'

'Don't be long.'

'I'm not going anywhere. You know that.'

She loved his company, his talk, even when he was wandering. She loved his stories of the past, and his mannerisms, even if he did rather play up to them. She noticed, for example, that he made wheezing noises as she came into the room and that they increased in volume as she started to approach his bed. She had come to love him most when he was being most difficult. Sometimes, straining to follow his line of thought, straining to hear him, she was worried he was fading, but then he would come storming back, as now:

'I know what comes next.'

'Well, sir, that's more than I do. What comes next then?'

'Place pill on tongue. Sip drink. Full steam ahead. Guns firing.'

'Exactly.'

He made his mock contrite face.

'Was I being ... obstreperous?'

'Well ...'

'Having a bit of a ding-dong, was I, when you came in? Bit of a how-d'you-do?'

She wiggled her head.

'A bit.'

'Was I? No need for you to tell Lady Churchill, I hope. Not getting out of hand, was I?'

'No, not out of hand. What about another poem? Would you like that?'

Ah, yes, he thought, the soothing balm of a story, a poem, a yarn, yes, we'll have my daily poem, but no sooner had he had the thought of a daily poem than he'd lost it, and instead he heard himself saying,

'Still, better than being a wet flannel, isn't it?'

'You never are. I don't think anyone could ever accuse you of being a wet flannel.'

A smile passed between them.

'But I don't want to end up in a straitjacket.'

'Please don't! It's not funny, sir. It's really not funny at all. It just upsets me. There's no chance of such a thing being done to you.'

'I suppose if I die it solves a lot of problems.'

'No one's thinking like that.'

'Oh, I bet they are. Waning powers. Death. A political death ... the big statue crashing down always cheers someone up. Someone goes down, Millie, someone goes up, that's the way of the world. Some people out there will be praying for my demise.'

'If that's so, it's not right.'

'But it's true. I'm history.'

'It's not right for a nurse to look at life like that. And I don't.'

He rubbed his trembling hands together, suddenly restless again.

'I must get back to painting. Daubing. Back to my studio. Set my easel up. Discovered it too late, you know, painting. I was forty-one. Forty years, half of my life was gone before I even started. What a fool I was.'

'I like the ones I've seen downstairs.'

'Do you? Thank you.'

'There's one of France, isn't there, by the sea in France. Or is that Italy? I've never been abroad.'

'Only daubs. Daubs. I'm not a real artist. But my brushes ... await me. You can daub anywhere, you know, Millie, you just put your easel up and splash in, that's the thing about it. Marrakech, Maidstone, it doesn't matter. But it's no good if ... it's no good if your hand is like ... this. No good if your paw is all of a tremble.'

'Let's hope you'll be painting again soon.'

He shook his head and his eyes flickered and started to close, then opened again.

'I'm told people give up smoking and drinking.'

'That's good, if they can bring themselves to do it.'

'They must want to live very much.'

'I want to live very much, don't you? And you're in charge of our country, sir.'

'However long I go on, though, I don't think I'll ever become venerable, do you?'

Nurse Appleyard wasn't sure she knew what 'venerable' meant.

'Can I get you anything? Anything that's allowed, that is.'

'Nothing that's allowed is much fun.'

'I wouldn't know about that.'

'I'd like a nasal spray.'

She couldn't help grinning.

'A nasal spray?'

'Is there a new nasal spray I can have?'

'I'll ask the doctor.'

'But please stay. Because I have an army of memories attacking me. In disorderly ranks.'

'Do you?'

'And I want you . . . to tell me something.'

'If I can.'

His eyes were clear.

'Can you . . . can you tell days apart, one from the other?'

'Days apart?'

'Because blowed if I can.'

'You're getting better every day, sir, and that's what matters to me, to all of us. Every day I can see an improvement in you. That's how I tell them apart.'

*

'How did you sleep?'

'Only too well.'

'You can't sleep too well, Winston. And you've been a bit up and down lately. Good days and bad days, eh?'

'I was a long long way away, Charles.'

'Never mind, we've all been waiting for you here. Haven't we, nurse?'

'We have, sir. Is there anything you want now?'

'No, thank you, nurse,' the doctor said. 'That'll be all for the moment.'

The two old men watched Nurse Appleyard walk across the bedroom in her upright way. And glide out of the room.

'Most lovely girl,' Winston said.

'She's a grand lass. And you are satisfied with her?'

'Range perfect. Visibility perfect.'

'Sorry?'

'If only we had some six-inch guns on board, eh?'

Moran grimaced and looked away.

'Yes, well, mm.'

It was a side of Winston he could do without.

'And I've had very bad dreams, Charles. Fearful muddle they were. Nothing you clever doctors can do about dreams, I suppose?'

'Not that I know about.'

'Bombers, Gallipoli, battleships, Japs, North Africa, Tobruk, the Blitz, I was all over the show. Not very good history.'

'That's dreams for you.'

'The *Prince of Wales* was sunk. And the *Repulse.* I sent them without air cover.'

Tears were, once again, not far away.

'Things go wrong in a long life, Winston. Even for you things can go wrong. You have achieved more than anyone else in the world.'

'Only to be brought down by conjunctivitis.'

'You haven't got conjunctivitis. Leave the medicine to me.'

'Yes, I have. Look!'

'Your eyes are red because you are tired.'

'I asked the nurse to give me a mirror.'

'Did you?'

'Yes. I looked into my glass, and viewed my wasting skin. Don't look so worried, Charles, that's a bit of poetry.'

'I wouldn't know.'

'Anyway, my eyes are itching. It's a microbe, I know it's a microbe, and I can feel them advancing in a hideous heel-clicking onslaught, brutish and vile, it's an imminent invasion, and I want all available resources mobilised to attack and outgun and destroy these bugs and the sons and grandsons of these bugs.'

'Well, one thing's clear. As you can now diagnose yourself *and* recite poetry, you must be getting better.'

'I am, that's my point!'

There was a noisy fly buzzing around the room, head-butting the window panes and every wall.

'Your words are back all right. Now we want to get these arms and legs moving. That is the next step. More mobility. Have you noticed any improvement there?'

'Charles, would you add another to all the kindnesses

you are heaping on my head and swat that fly. Just behind your shoulder.'

'Of course. Where is it? Ah, yes, there.'

The doctor rolled up a newspaper tightly, and to the Prime Minister's delight he started to move wildly around the room, making a number of increasingly comic lunges down and then up, backhands and overhead swipes.

'Ah, charades! Wimbledon? Is this Wimbledon?'

'Too quick for me, I'm afraid. Give up. Not as fit as I was. Where were we?'

'You were asking me about my legs and I was about to convey the good news that I am now ready to walk across the room.'

'No, you're not.'

'I am feeling forceful.'

'Not now.'

'I shall follow the established path the nurse takes to the door. I don't think things are coming on too badly, do you? I could settle for a kick in my gallop but I wouldn't want a wobble in my walk.'

'It's far too early, Winston. You might fall.'

'Watch this.'

He started to move his leg over the side of the bed.

'Don't!'

'Oh, don't be so defeatist, Charles! I'm not going to burst an artery, am I? Do try to keep things in proportion, and do remember that trees do not grow up to the sky. It's unlike you, all this sackcloth and ashes, because you are one of those in my orchestra whose note I value. So let's make hell while the sun shines, shall we, because I can still manage everything better than everyone else and I'm not going to quit. *Why am I loth to leave this earthly scene?* That's Burns. No, Barnes. Burns or Barnes. Anyway, someone needs to fight these damned Socialists. Who's going to deal with An-eur-in Bev-*an*?'

'You, by the sound of it.'

'Because no one else is. For a while it seems I lost the words, was played out, couldn't find the words when I wanted them, and I was a little scrambled, but listen to me now, and, what's more, and I don't mind telling you this, the more they hustle me the longer I'll stay. You can tell Anthony that I am better. As you are about to see when I walk across the room.'

'No, I am not about to see you walk across the room because you are not about to do it. And you can tell Anthony whatever you like when he returns.'

'You failed badly with the fly and have been sulking ever since, and now you can't even help me to get back on my feet. Or won't.'

'I'm helping you by saying no. N.O. spells no. Back in bed!'

The Prime Minister glared at his doctor, then banged his hand on the bed rest. The china rattled. He turned his face away. Neither man spoke, and it seemed their meeting was over, when there was a growl:

'Hair brush.'

'I'm sorry?'

'Hair brush! Pass it!'

'Don't talk to me like that, Winston.'

'Like what?'

'Don't you be Bolshie with me because I won't take it. I'm not your valet.'

'Would you please pass my hair brush?'

Moran handed it to him.

The Prime Minister made a token attempt at brushing the bits of hair left around his ears. Then the puff seemed to go out of him and he made a muffled sound which might, on a bad day, have passed for an apology.

'Winston?'

'What is it *now*!'

'You have not been well and you have been under great strain. You want me to get you back up on your feet and I am doing my very best.'

'It doesn't seem so to me. I am ... humiliated by my own decay.'

'I admire your guts and always have done and you are recovering well. But guts is one thing and foolishness is another. You are being arrogant and I am afraid to say you are at risk of becoming cocksure.'

'Oh, arrogant and cocksure, am I? Are you my medical adviser, Charles, or my travelling conscience? I'm never sure which.'

'You must follow my timetable.'

'In the meantime I could do with a cigar.'

'You know the answer.'

'A cigar helps one to face the general bloodiness of things.'

'Face it without.'

'The Filipinos are a very mild brand. There's a new box in my study, second drawer down in my desk.'

'Still no.'

'Self-expression is better than self-denial.'

'Sometimes.'

'You'd have made a good monk, Charles. Or a bishop. I have made more bishops than anyone since St Augustine.'

'I think you may have said that to me before.'

'I have smoked all my life and it's never done me any harm. I've probably said that to you before as well. In all probability there is not a thing I have said to you today or am going to say to you tomorrow that I haven't said before. Husbands and wives tend to understand that. I must check up with your wife, find out how original you are.'

'You're incorrigible. I give up.'

'You just need to ginger me up a bit. I need some of your red pills. They're the ones, the red ones. I call them Morans. Not the white ones.'

'I can give you red pills, Winston, but I do warn you off the red boxes.'

'So should I wave the yellow flag? Do a Singapore? Eh? Run away? That's your view, is it? Or another Tobruk? How about a bit of courage and a few red pills? As a recipe?'

In spite of himself, Moran was amused. How often Winston's humour saved the day.

'Honestly, you and your pills.'

'How many do you think I've taken, over the years?'

'More than I've had hot dinners.'

'Can you remember them all?'

Moran counted on his fingers:

'Phergan, Bellergal, aminophyline, Disprins, Immenoctal and Seconal. Red and white.'

'You see? And here I am.'

'You're not easy to help, are you?'

'We need a lighthouse flashing. That is what works in politics. We need a song that everyone can hum.'

'So they say.'

'And only I can do that.'

'No one does it better, I agree.'

'As we'll see at Margate.'

'Margate?'

He beckoned Moran closer.

'For your private ear.'

'Yes?'

'The Party Conference.'

'Yes?'

'In Margate.'

'Is that where it is?'

'In October.'

'Ah. And does Jock know what you are planning?'

'As much as he needs to for the present.'

'I see.'

'But whatever you do, don't tell Clemmie.'

*

That is unusual.

Jock Colville looked up from his huge pile of papers, in the midst of sorting them neatly into two trays, Yes or No – yes, those to mention to the Prime Minister, and no, those for another day – and saw Nurse Appleyard outside. He could not remember ever having seen her beyond the four walls of the house, indeed rarely outside the close quarters of the Prime Minister's small bedroom. Perhaps in the earliest period of the crisis it had been considered imperative, on security grounds, that she kept focused on her job and did not mix at all with the other staff. But as the weeks passed the tension and the jumpiness had eased somewhat, with the general tone becoming noticeably more relaxed.

Anyway, there she was, out there on her own, with her eyes down, walking along the garden path.

In fact, there was something altogether unusual about Nurse Appleyard. At first, he had to admit, Colville had found her floating status in Chartwell difficult to grasp, let alone endorse, and that was still partly true, but one had to accept that it was how the elastically unconventional Churchills had always operated.

Moran spoke highly of her, too, which was rare enough from the old grouser, while Nurse Appleyard seemed to have found a tactful and accommodating *modus vivendi* with Lady Churchill, when things in that territorial department could so easily have become explosive.

In fact, looking out at the garden, Colville suddenly felt like a breather himself. He put notice of Eisenhower's crisis conference on Korea firmly in the No tray, screwed the top back on his fountain pen and left by the back door just as Nurse Appleyard was cresting the slope. Normally the picture of health, she was looking very pale and her eyes were strained.

'A penny for your thoughts, nurse.'

'Oh, Mr Colville, I didn't see you.'

'Enjoying the garden, are we?'

'You couldn't not enjoy this place, could you?'

'It's a handsome house all right.'

'It's like being in a film.'

'I suppose it is.'

'And the doctor told me to get out into the fresh air for an hour.'

Colville fell in step with her.

'Do you mind if we walk together for a little?'

Nurse Appleyard was taken aback.

'If you like, sir.'

'I'm not intruding?'

'No, not at all.'

'And your impatient patient is safe and sound on his own for the moment?'

'Oh, I'm sure he is.'

'Excellent.'

'Well, he was fine when I slipped out, and the doctor said he would be looking in.'

They walked on.

'You have certainly been on duty for very long spells at a time.'

'That's not unusual for a nurse, sir.'

'But shouldn't you be having some days off? The last thing we want is for you to become unwell. Shall I have a word on your behalf with Lord Moran?'

'No, thank you, but it's nice of you to think of it.'

'You're sure?'

'I'm sure. I'd much rather be here until we've seen him through. I don't want to leave him.'

Colville was touched. She really was rather splendid and had spoken for all of them. *I'd much rather be here until we've seen him through. I don't want to leave him.* He slowed in his walk, wishing he could think of something else to say to her, wishing he could reply in kind, wishing he could keep it going. But as he strode on nothing came to mind.

He should be getting back, but he was determined not to miss this opportunity. He stopped and faced her.

'I don't quite know how you have managed it, nurse, but you do seem to have helped keep the Prime Minister on an even keel. Indeed buoyant. That has been apparent to everyone. And I would like you to know that everyone hugely appreciates it. We have all been most impressed.'

She was surprised and on the edge of finding it funny, the way he said things, the words he chose, *even keel* and *buoyant.*

'He's getting better, Mr Colville, and that's the main thing.'

'How long do you imagine it will be before he'll be out here for a walk with you?'

'You'd better ask the doctor that, sir. It is not for me to say.'

'Of course, I quite understand.'

'I'm sure the doctor will explain.'

Colville, not at all sure the doctor would, looked back at the house.

'Well, I'm afraid my desk calls. But what a stroke of good fortune that we bumped into each other.'

As he finished his sentence, Colville nodded in his rather serious way, and left her. Millie, smiling to herself, resumed her walk. A bit further on she saw a wheelbarrow on the side of the lawn, and in the flower bed beyond one of the gardeners was head down, rump up. She called out.

'Hullo, is that you, Tom?'

He straightened up. When he saw who it was his countryman's face, as brown as a berry, beamed.

'Hullo there, Millie.'

'Nice day.'

'It is that. Day off then?'

'You're joking, I'm a nurse.'

'Nev-er!'

'What are you up to then?'

'Just sorting out this bed. Then that big one over there.'

'I suppose that's what we both do, isn't it?'

'What's that?'

'Sort out the beds.'

'Yeah, you're right there, Millie.'

She took in the view.

'So, how long have you worked here, Tom?'

'Since I was fourteen. Left school and came here.'

'That's a spell.'

'Never worked anywhere but Chartwell, never wanted to, never will.'

'Meant to ask, how did you get on last Saturday? Cricket? The big match?'

'Oh, over at Penshurst. Yes, got a few.'

'Well done.'

'Then had a wild swipe, didn't I? Rush of blood. Same old story. Put a spinner on and I'll have a swipe.'

They both laughed.

'Never mind. Did you win, though?'

'Yeah, that's the main thing, isn't it? As long as you win. You can't beat that feeling.'

'I think we're winning too,' she said quietly, her eyes flicking up the slope.

'Up in the house?'

'Yes.'

Tom nodded slowly at her, then looked around him. Her heart jumped. Had she said more than she should? How much did the gardeners know?

'That's good to hear. When he was a bit younger he used to come down here a fair bit, often just before we went home, take off his coat and roll up his sleeves and get stuck in. Seemed to love it.'

'Probably took his mind off things.'

'Always telling you what to do, mind, do this do that, always had to have his own way, had to be boss!'

'Oh, I bet!'

'I miss him around the place, though. A lot of this garden is down to him.'

*

He'd had his sights on the wheelchair or, as he called it, the old jalopy, for quite a while. It had been in the corner of his eye ever since he came round and rejoined the land of the living. The old jalopy was parked up against the wall opposite, to the right of the bedroom window. It was, Winston judged, five or six paces away from his bed. He measured it again in his mind's eye. Six paces at most. Or seven short steps. If he could take them. If, that is, his tottery legs held up.

Once he was sitting in the wheelchair he could rest a bit, have a change of view, then see if he could move himself around. He had to be careful, though. First of all he had to reach it and get into it, then he could get the feel of it and be back in bed in no time.

And the wheelchair brought back his dear comrade FDR. If Franklin D. Roosevelt could carry out the arduous duties of President of the United States from a wheelchair, with not a trace of self-pity, then the least the Prime Minister of the United Kingdom could do was take a quick spin round in the safety of his small bedroom.

The strategic plan was simple enough, but the execution might well be more tricky. Above all, he didn't want to be spotted. To be caught in the act by Nurse Appleyard wouldn't be too bad. Nurse Appleyard would understand because Millie-Molly-Mandy was on his side. Moran would flare up, of course. He'd boil over. But he would soon enough see the thinking, and what motive lay behind it.

Clementine, however, would be a complete disaster. Jaguars and trees didn't begin to capture the full flavour. The riot act would be read.

Face that if it happened.

Time to concentrate on strategy.

Because these things took time. Rome, as he often said, dear old Rome, wasn't built in a day. Nor were the *Nar-zees* defeated overnight. Nor Everest climbed in a hurry. Because you needed to establish base camps. You needed to plan ahead, one thing at a time. Best thing was to do it in stages, each step a step closer, inch up on them, but once you had decided on the final assault you must take your courage in both hands and go hell for leather. That's what he always said to Monty, to all of them, to all his generals and chiefs.

You mustn't fall short.

If they can climb Everest, you can reach FDR.

Steel yourself and think only of victory.

How did that thing . . . that saying go?

Every day
In every way
I'm getting better
And better.

So said . . . Monsieur Coué. Quite right too. Perseverance was the way. A dose of self-administered optimism. Imagine the desired result. Coué was the chap's name. Kooo-ayyy. Emile Coué. An auto-suggestive frog from Nancy. A Nancy boy frog. No, Winston, that's not very edifying.

Still, even though I've had a good sleep I'm really only half awake. You shouldn't judge me when I'm half awake. I used to wake up feeling there was half a bottle of champagne inside me. No longer. But I am, you'll agree, in much better shape, you can tell I'm more myself the last day or two. More bite in my jaw, more grip in my paw. Today I could enjoy giving someone a good kicking, Aneurin Bevan for a start, the Honourable Member for Ebbw Vale.

Listen?

No sound outside the door.

Not a squeak on the staircase.

FDR would be watching him from up there. And approving.

Go!

He lowered his right leg over the side of the bed. Then, carefully, his left. There wasn't much feeling in it. Some, but not much. Lower it very carefully, as nursey showed him. Seated on the side of the bed, he rocked backwards and forwards slowly, building up more rhythm and speed, until, gripping the side table with his right hand and pressing down, he took a deep breath and tried with all his might to lift his backside off the bed, yes, you're half up, keep going, yes, yes—

Only to land back with a bump.

Bugger.

He took some more deep breaths. He wasn't at his best. He was at his worst between lunch and half past three. It was now half past two. That explained it. The torpor. His heart needed to settle. You could see why cripples wanted to bump themselves off. No, stop that, that's not very edifying either.

Five deep breaths. In, out.

And then go again.

Go!

Arms straining, jaw set, eyes closed tight he tried again, this time somehow becoming more or less upright if still bent over. He was upright but stooped. Stooped but upright. If wobbly. He stood there, swaying, unsteady, a tree in a storm, tilting, listing to port.

Deep breaths.

He then made a gesture forward but his foot did not move. He had sent it a clear message, had he not? Send it again! It stayed where it was. Disobeyed orders. Hopeless foot. Bloody hopeless foot. But he was still upright, wasn't he, that was the big thing, and he was buggered if he was going to be beaten by this or any other foe, let alone sit down.

No thought of withdrawal. Reissue command.

Move!

And his foot did move, this time it did move, now you're moving, that's it, we're off, like a stork, now you're walking, except he wasn't so much walking as tottering and stumbling, not so much stumbling as plunging head first, like a man about to take a determined dive into a swimming pool, but he made the distance across the floor and half turned just in time to plonk his backside down in the wheelchair, in FDR, albeit banging the old jalopy hard into the wall.

There was a loud bump.

He listened, his heart going double time.

The game was up.

They must have heard.

Must have.

But . . . no one came running.

He soon got the drift of the wheelchair, and moved it, inched it forward, then it rolled and he found he was touching the bookcase. He had crossed the room; he had crossed the Rubicon. He looked back at his bed, turning the wheelchair slowly, reversing slowly, before moving into forward gear and returning to the parking place.

All right, you couldn't call it a spin exactly but it was a damn sight better than being in bed.

Five more deep breaths.

And he re-gathered his strength.

He stood up. More upright this time. And shuffled and launched himself back across the room. Left, right, left, right. On his way back to his bed, however, his left big toe caught the edge of the carpet as if it were a tripwire, he buckled and fell heavily, face first.

Bugger.

His knees hit the floor hard, but his upper body landed on the bed.

He was winded but he clung to his position, he held his

position, and did not slide further down. His stomach hurt. His chest hurt. His arms hurt.

Straining hard, it took him fully five minutes to lever, squirm, wriggle and tug himself up to a bending crouch. Many had died in such an attempt. Base camp, then on the South Col route. You passed dead bodies and their unseen souls on the way up. But he had established his footholds.

He rested, breathing hard, within sight of the summit. No one in the history of mankind had ever done this before. There was only the final push left, one more huge effort and he could plant the Union Jack and bury a cross in the snow before descending.

Snow blind, but clinging on hard to the flag, he closed his eyes. He opened his eyes and peered through his goggles and dug his fingers in and tested his grip and took the strain and tugged himself up and up and over and on to the top of the bed, where he lay face down in the soft white pillow, short of oxygen, panting hard, and muttering to himself in triumph.

*

Progress is slow but steady.

That was the quotidian phrase used, in great secrecy, in the smallest of circles on both sides of the Atlantic. Eden knew of Churchill's plight; Churchill knew of Eden's. Letters and cables marked *Private and Confidential*, messages from loyal lieutenants, arrived at both addresses. Both men had motivation aplenty to hide their incapacities and to regain full health as quickly as possible, to show their stamina and to demonstrate their powers of recovery, to keep the show on the road, to protect their position, but whatever gloss you put on it, progress in both places was slow but steady.

Both men had taken severe blows.

When you look back on a protracted illness it does not seem to have lasted so very long. You're not even sure what all the fuss was about. At the time, however, when pessimism comes to call on the land of the infirm, with each day tedious and improvement apparently negligible, it can feel as if there is no end in sight. Moods come and are often slow to go. Such spells call for a different kind of courage.

In July the Prime Minister said, 'I am not enjoying July.'

In August he said, 'I am not enjoying August.'

On both sides of the Atlantic small, slow steps were, however, taken. In Boston the Foreign Secretary, though unhealthy in pallor, started to eat the lightest of meals. He drank more milk. His insides felt a little stronger. He sat in the garden under the hot Massachusetts sun and read, as he often did, *The Histories* of Herodotus. He put on a pound, possibly two, in weight.

Still unwell and sporadically fretful, Mr Eden planned his return trip with the utmost care. The voyage on HMS *Surprise* would take him, as a guest of the Navy, on a cruise to Malta, Palermo and Athens, and then around his beloved Greek islands. Greece would be the final stage of his convalescence, Greece, with plenty of swimming and sun and seafood: kalamari, lavraki, and gavros with peppers. By then his stomach would surely be fine and his meals more substantial. When he arrived back in London in late September or early October (his aides, worried about the damaging length of his absence, urged an earlier return) he would be fighting fit and ready to take over the reins. Within a month or two he would be settled into Number 10, where he belonged.

In Chartwell the Prime Minister found he was able to concentrate for longer periods. He picked up and re-read Disraeli's *Coningsby*. More excitingly, he was able, with the help of a stick, to walk haltingly across the slightly uneven floor of his bedroom. Then, one fine morning, he was without a stick. Then, one wet afternoon, when a bad mood had come to stay, Winston had a blazing row with his doctor.

'Throw that damn thing out!' he roared, pointing at the wheelchair.

Then the great day arrived when the Prime Minister was ready, with help on all sides, to go downstairs, sideways, step by painful step: a great day but by any standards a slow descent to ground level.

Old friends started to come to Chartwell, the Churchills 'had company over', and it felt more like the old days: a good supper, a good few glasses of Pol Roger, and talking late, often far too late for Winston's health.

Next stop was a short walk in the garden on the arm of his wife or, more often, on the arm of his rather splendid nurse. On the horizon lay croquet. Not a word of all this, of course, got into any of the daily papers. Not a word about illness, not the word caretaker, not the word successor, nothing. Mum was still the word.

*

One bright morning the Prime Minister was sitting on a bench on the north terrace, talking of this and that (politics mostly) to Jock Colville. Getting the lie of the land. Things were bad in Burma, things were even worse in Egypt – trouble was brewing in Cairo – and there was yet more violence in Kashmir. Not to mention the situation in Persia and Indo-China.

'Perhaps I'm asking too much, Jock, but is there by any chance any good news?'

'Yes, we won the Ashes. At the Oval yesterday. Compton and Edrich were mobbed as they ran *orf*.'

'So I heard. Marvellous.'

That was the moment he saw her light step, her upright posture, as she came across the lawn. They had agreed to meet when she was ready.

'Jock, could I ask you to give me a few moments alone?'

'Of course.'

'There's more to say on so many issues, so you will come back, won't you?'

'Absolutely.'

She smiled at them both.

'Good morning, sir. Good morning, Mr Colville.'

'Good morning, nurse,' Jock said, sliding away. 'Would you both excuse me?'

'Do sit down for a moment, Millie.'

'Thank you, sir.'

They sat side by side, the Prime Minister and his nurse, and looked over the swimming pool and the lakes.

'It's time for me to go now, sir.'

'I know.'

'I don't want to.'

'And I don't want you to. Back to your hospital, is it?'

'Yes, I'm reporting to Matron and I'll be back on duty tomorrow morning.'

'Will you?'

'Tomorrow morning, first thing.'

'No days off, no holiday first?'

'No, but it's never too bad once you start, is it, and I'll see some of my friends again. And that'll be nice.'

'What would we do without friends?'

She turned to face him.

'I've loved being here. In Chartwell.'

'You have?'

'I've loved every minute. You've all been so kind. I'll never forget it. And thank you, sir. I've learnt so much from you.'

He tried to speak but he could not.

'And it's so wonderful seeing you up and about and back on your feet.'

He nodded.

'I hate . . . goodbyes,' he managed.

'Oh, so do I.'

She got her handkerchief out of her handbag. His hand clumsily brushed hers.

'I couldn't have done it without you, Millie. And, if I may, I would like to give you something, as a very small token of my gratitude.'

He picked up a parcel off the bench beside him. She put her hand to her mouth.

'What is it?'

'Close your eyes and feel the shape. Not too difficult to guess, surely?'

He handed her the parcel.

'Thank you. How lovely.'

'I'm not responsible for the beautiful wrapping, of course, that is my wife's doing, and I'm not sure how you feel about opening presents in front of the giver, it does put rather unfair pressure on both parties, but I would on this very special occasion appreciate it if you were kind enough to open it now.'

'If you'd like me to.'

She started slowly to unwrap it, being very careful not to tear the paper.

'You can even smell it if you wish.'

She laughed and continued the unwrapping. It was a copy of *The Oxford Book of English Verse*, edited by Sir Arthur Quiller-Couch. She opened the front cover. Inside, on the title page, he had written:

'To Millie, with heartfelt thanks, Winston S. Churchill.'

And, for the briefest of seconds, he pressed her hand.

*

Two weeks or so later the Prime Minister went up to Yorkshire, to Doncaster, to watch the St Leger. This was against Clementine's strong advice. The Prime Minister and his wife, not for the first time, had words. She told him she feared he might suffer a setback on the longish and very public walk he would have to make to the paddock: that it was premature, and he should not be profligate with his resources. He brushed this aside. She accused him of becoming increasingly immune to political *and* medical advice.

Winston was, however, determined to join the Queen and Prince Philip at Doncaster and join them he did. He watched the race with them, before travelling on from Yorkshire, once more against Lady Churchill's wishes, in the royal train to Balmoral. The Prime Minister found the Queen an absolute poppet but the overnight train trip to Deeside, as Clementine had predicted, left him exhausted and flat.

On 17 September, while the Foreign Secretary was cruising around the Greek islands (and longing for the Prime Minister to go, as go he surely would), the Prime Minister himself was taking a late holiday in the south of France. He was staying at La Capponcina, the villa of Lord Beaverbook, one of the three men who had met in Chartwell and paced the lawn so early that morning.

Promising his wife he would keep out of the casinos, Churchill put on his ten-gallon hat and packed his paintbox – his joyride, his hobby and his greatest distraction – in case the moment came when he felt like plunging into a daub. He also took the proofs of *The English-Speaking Peoples*. Clementine did not accompany him, preferring the peace of Chartwell to the glitz of the Riviera, so it was his loyal private secretary, Jock Colville, who followed the Prime Minister to the colonnades of Cap d'Ail.

By turns irritable or placid, cantankerous or genial, muddled or clear-headed, Churchill sat by the great stone fireplace or outside looking at the sea, nodding off in the soft relaxing air of the Mediterranean, smoking his cigar and brooding on his fate and the future. With the vultures circling, could he wrestle again with public life? Could he get a grip of everything, grip everything firmly, and still master the complexities?

Yes, he could.

The world needed patience. Yes, he might feel a little torpor after luncheon, never the best time of day for him, but the world needed experience, his experience. When summoned to the telephone to take a call from Kent he said he found it difficult to hear Clementine's voice, though the deafness may have been strategic.

While in La Capponcina he dictated – his handwriting was still very shaky – two thousand words of his speech for Margate. It was very much a first draft, and not yet up to scratch, but the first shot was always the most difficult part. And, above all, he had the big idea which every speech needs, the flashing lighthouse, the idea which sets the pulse racing. Feeling all the better for having the rough version under his belt, he stood up, straightened up, pulled back his shoulders, chin up, no slouching, poured himself a fortifier, put on his hat and picked up his paintbox.

He padded around, talking to himself:

The French have taste in all they do
While we are quite without;
For Nature, who to them gave goût
To us gave only gout.

On the edge of the terrace he found the right view and the right spot and set up his easel. He looked up; he looked down. The sky was blue and there was the blue paint. He splashed into the turpentine and he walloped into the blue and he worked with a berserk fury, his veins bursting with pleasure, until the canvas was cowering.

By sundown he was well on his way to a picture of the rocks and the pine trees and the sea. But, with that tell-tale tremble in his paw, he could see it wasn't very good.

*

Holidays in the south of France and Greece have to end.

As does convalescence.

The meeting with the Foreign Secretary, which had to come sooner or later, took place at the very end of September. Outside, in the garden of 10 Downing Street, the air was chill and a few early leaves were falling, and the dew now took all morning to clear from the lawn. Some days it did not clear at all.

Though they masked their reactions, both of them

were shocked at the man they saw walking towards them. Churchill, despite his time on the terrace at Cap d'Ail, was pasty and hunched – and had even more watery eyes. On top of this, he seemed to favour one foot. Eden, though deeply suntanned from his hours on deck, was even thinner, as gaunt as ever and noticeably frail. His suit jacket appeared now to hang on his shoulders.

'Anthony, my dear boy.'

'Winston.'

Churchill warmly took his hand and held his arm for a while.

'Anthony.'

'Well, here we are, Winston.'

'And what a business.'

'As you say, what a business.'

'Indeed.'

'But you're all patched up, Anthony?'

'Oh, I feel absolutely fine. The episode is behind me. I am nearly one hundred per cent.'

'And the American chappie? As good with the knife as he's cracked up to be?'

'Dr Cattell was quite superb. As were his whole team at the Lahey Clinic. The Americans could not have been kinder.'

Jokingly, Eden gestured as if to pull out his shirt:

'Would you like me to show you the quality of his work?'

'No, no, I have no wish to see your wound, dear boy, but it's so good that you feel you are on the mend. All I would ask, all I would beg, is that you do nurse your strength. You can't be too careful with these things, you know.'

Then he pointed at him with his cigar.

'And you do, forgive me, need a little more weight.'

'A little, perhaps. But I'm on a strict diet, and I've always been lean.'

'And I confess I need a little less, but can you imagine life without beefsteak pie?'

To prove his point the Prime Minister slapped the waistcoat on his wobbly stomach, and kept slapping his paunch:

'I know, I really should cut down and get myself in shape for the tenth.'

'The tenth?'

'It's been so long, though, since we met.'

'Three months. And how are things with *you* now, Winston?'

'Back in harness, and a good report from Charles. A clean bill of health.'

'But it was touch and go for a while?'

'Was it?'

'By all accounts?'

The Prime Minister's fingernails tapped the top of the table.

'Charles hasn't been indiscreet, I hope? No loose talk?'

'No, this concern was all from Jock.'

'That's kind of him, but he's very young. It was just the sort of challenge I like, the enemy attacking on a broad front and me running the gauntlet. Then, just when they think they're winning, back comes the decisive counter-attack. Never mistreat your enemies by halves, Anthony.'

A touch ruefully, the Foreign Secretary, who had noticed that the Prime Minister's lisp was now even more liquid, said he would bear that in mind, adding,

'But July and August can't have been easy, Winston, with you locked up and *hors de combat* in Chartwell.'

'I did not enjoy July, Anthony, but we did beat the Australians in August—'

'Indeed, by eight wickets, I hear.'

'And I was not exactly – no doubt to Clementine's dismay – locked up. As for *hors de combat*, never!'

'I was in jest.'

'Of course you were. But the great thing is, Anthony, we kept it all under wraps and out of the papers. Not a squeak was heard, not a funeral note as his corset to the rampart we hurried. The Beaver played an absolute blinder, as did Camrose and Bracken, all three of them came up trumps.'

'Indeed, you sat on the story. So Jock told me. Beautifully handled.'

Winston lumbered to the side table.

'Would you like a whisky and soda? Mmmm? Come on.'

'Not just at the moment, thank you. A bit early for me.'

'No, you're right, probably better not, one thing at a time, eh? But you're feeling fit and ready for the fray?'

'Perfectly.'

'Splendid.'

'Which is just as well, as our party machine needs reform from top to bottom. Before we go into the next election under a new leader.'

'Our party machine needs reforming? Does it really? Can't we just get on with things?'

The Foreign Secretary could not keep the edge from his voice.

'No, we've neglected things for far too long, it's all become too hotchpotch for my taste. I've spoken at some length to Rab and to Mac about it and we all agree. Morale is low, and we are entering another political world.'

The Prime Minister picked up a glass tumbler.

'Because I'll quite understand, Anthony, if, in view of your most difficult last few months, you feel unable to continue. At the Foreign Office, I mean.'

Eden very nearly snorted but he swallowed hard and managed to make no sound. A poisoned silence ensued. When Eden did speak it was quietly, even deadpan, though if you were close enough you might just have seen the moustache on his upper lip tremble.

'At the Foreign Office?'

'Because no one has ever filled it with more distinction. No one. As I was saying to Rab only the other day, the Foreign Office, in all its long and chequered career, has never been better led than by Anthony. Never.'

Eden reached out for the arm of a chair, and gripped it. He looked as if he had taken a heavy punch to his solar plexus, paralysing his diaphragm, the blow landing right on top of his wound, right on top of the recent repair work. So. So, they were not about to fix a date. Yet again there was to be no handover. No retirement. The old man was going on, as Macmillan had always predicted he would, going on and on until the pub closed. This was not the moment to force a showdown, but why, Eden thought, why do I get all the knocks?

'May I sit down?'

'Oh, please do. Do.'

'In other words, Winston, you are content to go on?'

'*We* go on as we were, Anthony. Yes, you and I together. The best team. KBO. KBO, eh?'

'I never imagined this. Never in my wildest dreams. Not even as I walked into the room.'

'And when you've fully recovered, when you're looking better, we'll have a good long talk and clarify things.'

'Things already seem perfectly clear.'

'Meanwhile, let's see how things stand after the Conference, shall we?'

'After Margate?'

'Because if the brute isn't competent at Margate, if I can't do it on the tenth, I won't carry on and they can put me out to grass.'

Eden's voice was now deeply weary, though still tart.

'Unless your doctor persuades you to continue, or you find some other pretext. Surely this is the time, you've had a wonderfully long and successful innings. And if you leave now you will have so much to look back on.'

'But I still feel I can be of some use. And I am worried about you, Anthony, you're not too good. Look, are you sure you won't have a small one?'

'Quite sure.'

'As you wish. Just a drop for me then.'

The Prime Minister poured himself a decent glass.

'And a splash!'

The soda siphon hissed and bubbled. The Prime Minister raised his glass to his smouldering Foreign Secretary.

'Happy days!'

*

Like many an Englishman, Lord Moran did like to be beside the seaside. Like many an Englishman he was also particularly fond of it out of season, the bleakness of it, but he had never before been to Margate, nor for that matter anywhere else on the east Kent coast.

On the morning train down – in the carriage with Clementine, Colville and Charles – Winston gave the three of them one of his little history lessons, as was his wont. The Isle of Thanet, Winston explained, was the area in Kent where Hengist and Horsa began the Anglo-Saxon invasion in the fifth century. Then, at the very end of the sixth century St Augustine, the great Christian missionary, you've heard of him I hope, Charles, St Augustine landed near here on the Kentish coast after a voyage from Rome (Winston tended to get the Romans into everything). And of course Turner, the painter J.M.W. Turner, loved the light at Margate.

The Prime Minister glanced around the carriage. All three of them were looking out of the window at the flat landscape.

'No one seems remotely interested in a single word I have said.' And he started to sing 'Ole Man River'.

'Why don't you rest your voice, dear?' Clementine said. 'Save it for later.'

'Perhaps I am history as well now?'

'Not once they've heard your speech,' Jock said.

'Ah, yes, Charles. Talking of which, I need to share an idea with you. Well, Rab Butler's idea in fact. You know Rab, he does love an idea.'

'Oh, yes, and what's that?'

Not ten minutes earlier Moran had passed the preoccupied Chancellor of the Exchequer, with the world on his shoulders, in the corridor of the train.

'Rab suggests that I deliver my speech while sitting on a high stool.'

'Good God, no!'

'He suggests we have a stool ready on stage. Just in case.'

'No,' Moran said. 'That's the last thing you want.'

'I have to say I rather agree with Charles,' Colville said. 'That's exactly the view I take.'

Surprised by Colville's support, Moran went on even more strongly:

'It's what your enemies in the papers will love. It's the only thing they will latch on to. Packed hall, with everyone there, and there is the Prime Minister sitting on a saloon bar stool. No, no, no. A man who can't stand up can't run the country. That's the headline you'll get in the dirty dailies.'

Churchill clapped his hands together.

'And *that's* why you're in my orchestra, Charles, because the overall sound is always better with you. That's exactly the tune I wanted to hear.'

Clementine leant forward and spoke quietly, almost exclusively, to her husband:

'But you're sure, you're quite sure, you can stand for a full fifty minutes? Men much younger than you would struggle to do that.'

'Is that the length of the speech?' Moran asked.

'Yes.'

'*Fifty* minutes?'

'Yes,' Clementine said. 'He's timed it. Twice.'

'Oratory,' Winston said, 'is the art of successful dilution. Lloyd George said that. By the way, Charles, can you tell me why he died?'

'Who?'

'Lloyd George. There wasn't anything wrong with him, as far as I know.'

'It happens.'

'Very comforting of you. It isn't a perfect speech, this one, I know that, but I did send Jock on the most punitive cliché hunt.'

'I'm sure it will go down very well,' Colville said.

'Mind you, Clemmie, you are – as so often – right, I haven't been on my pins for that long since it happened. But I have practised the speech in front of a mirror.'

'Not standing up,' Clementine said.

'Not exactly standing up, no.'

'Sitting down, in fact.'

'Yes, sitting down, dear, as you say.'

'And that, Charles, goes some way to justifying Rab's concern. I do know it goes against the grain with you, Winston, it does with all of us, but much better to be safe than sorry. A discreet stool might be sensible.'

'How can a stool be discreet? This is absurd! I am no philosopher but a stool is a stool is a stool, and either it is there or it isn't.'

'How has your voice been?' Moran asked.

'Forceful,' Clementine said, 'as you can hear.'

'Excellent,' the doctor said.

'We are not concerned about your voice at the moment, Winston, we are concerned about your legs.'

'And I've been gargling every morning and every night. As directed.'

'I can certainly vouch for *that*,' Clementine added, *sotto voce*.

The Prime Minister started to dab the corner of his watery eyes with his handkerchief. Moran asked him,

'What time did you get to bed last night?'

'Late.'

'How late?'

'Pretty late.'

'After midnight?'

'A quarter to two.'

'It won't do!' Moran said. 'It won't do at all!'

Churchill waved all this away.

'And before the speech today, before walking on to the stage this afternoon, I am going to eat three mouthfuls of steak, a dozen oysters and take a half glass of champagne. At noon, that will be. That should do the trick.'

'You don't think that's rather overdoing it, my dear?'

'Overdoing it?'

'Yes.'

'Surely you expect me to eat my luncheon before I meet the party faithful in the Winter Gardens in Margate?'

'One could eat a more modest one.'

'One could, but I never have,' Winston said, decisively banging his seat, 'and I never will.'

At which point they all fell silent. Each sat alone with his or her anxieties, until, with the train approaching Margate and the sea a gun-metal grey, Charles said to the Prime Minister,

'Gloomy old day out there, I'm afraid.'

No, Winston shook his head, no no, not gloomy, and raised a hand, a sign they had come to know, as he intoned:

And not by eastern windows only,
When daylight comes, comes in the light;
In front the sun climbs slow, how slowly!
But westward, look, the land is bright!

'Arthur Hugh Clough, isn't it?' Jock said.

'Exactly, Jock. Which school did you go to?'

*

Reason has a hard time when anxiety and anticipation hold court.

A few hours later and Moran had never been so on edge. It was as if he was back pacing the touchline again, with five long minutes left on the watch till the final whistle, and the game could still go either way. Or he was about to sit his final examinations, with all his medical ambitions at stake. Or he was in the trenches again. No, nothing was that bad.

Clementine had not been able to sit down since setting foot in Margate. Well, she did very often take a seat, only, within a minute, to stand straight back up again and start walking about. When people spoke to Lady Churchill she appeared – and this was rare for her – not to hear. All day she had been quite unable to swallow more than a mouthful or two of food.

The Prime Minister's speech to the conference was five minutes away.

'Five minutes,' Jock Colville said, cool, calm and collected.

'My speech, where is it?'

'In your pocket. Your speech is in your pocket.'

The Prime Minister slapped himself.

'So it is.'

To cover all eventualities, Colville also had a copy of the speech in his own pocket, and he would be following it word for word.

'All the very best, darling. I know you will be wonderful.'

'Thank you, Cat dear.'

He started to sing Gracie Fields, very badly:

'*Wish me luck as you wave me good-bye, cheerio, here I go—*'

'Yes, good luck, Prime Minister.'

'Thank you, Jock, I'll do my best. Where will Charles be?'

'In the front row. Next to me.'

As he had arranged, at noon the Prime Minister did eat those three mouthfuls of steak and a dozen oysters, and he did indeed drink – it has to be said a rather generous – half glass of Pol Roger. Then, in a quick gulp of water, without Clementine spotting it, he swallowed one of his favourite red pills, his trump card, one of his standbys, one of his Major Morans. So when he arrived on stage, right on time, when he emerged from the wings with his white handkerchief in his breast pocket, there was no discernible kick in his gallop or waddle in his walk: he was pepped up and ready for the off.

Moran was braced in his seat. Row A, seat 40. That was front row left as you faced the platform, at the very end, next to the gangway and right next to the steps up to the platform, so that, should there be any crisis, he could be quickly at the Prime Minister's side. There was a cardboard notice hung on the chair.

Reserved for Lord Moran.

He was there in his role as Churchill's doctor, but he

was there just as much as an old friend, as a comrade-in-arms, and as an extremely biased supporter. He was the Prime Minister's sick-bed confessor, a follower, a fan, and one (he hoped) of the inner circle.

Moran's would be mainly a watching brief. He knew he would not be able to concentrate on precisely what the Prime Minister's arguments were, but truth to tell he didn't give a thrupenny bit one way or the other about the party political arguments or the government's policies. What the Prime Minister said, the sentences, the substance, would effectively wash over him, in one ear and out the other. He left all that to Jock and the politicians. The doctor was assessing his patient, the Prime Minister, as if the intellectual volume was turned off. Words, words, words. It was important for Moran only to focus on the level of his articulation, on the clarity of his voice, as well as the figure Winston cut, how the stooped body and the old carcass struck one as he stood there alone at the lectern.

For Clementine the next forty-nine minutes would be vicarious pain. With her tummy rumbling, she knew she would suffer every word of every sentence, and walk with him every step of the way. Each word, each step was a potential trap or an invisible tripwire. From the second Winston rose to speak, putting on his glasses and taking up his stance, that combative stance she knew and loved so well, her heart was driving wildly, careering all over the road.

Colville, calm and very still, was watching him like a hawk.

Across the whole width of the stage, high above the Prime Minister's head, was a huge banner reading ONWARD.

Did Winston wobble or sway as he got to his feet?

Clementine thought so.

Jock thought not. He's fine. He's sure-footed enough.

Did he look very stiff?

A bit, his wife thought.

Was that stiffness apparent to all?

If you did not know about the July stroke, did he look fine?

Or normal-ish? Difficult one.

What was normal-ish for an abnormal seventy-eight-year-old Prime Minister?

Yes, he looks his age, Moran thought, but don't we all?

He's slurring, Clementine felt. Yes, he's slurring.

Yes, Colville noticed, he was slurring and lisping. A bit.

But was he slurring and lisping any more than usual?

The best thing was, and they all felt this very strongly and they all felt it at the same time, the best thing was that the Prime Minister raised an immediate laugh. Getting a laugh early on was always a good sign if you were singing for your supper, because as soon as the audience (on whatever pretext) laughed the speaker and the listeners could both relax a little. Once the warm wave came back at you, your spirits were lifted, they were with you, lifting you, potentially with you. After that you were launched and they were yours to keep or to lose.

And the ripple, the laugh?

Retold cold it didn't add up to all that much, but the

point was it worked. The Prime Minister told them that he realised he had not spoken for a while, and that it was (pause) the first time in his political life (pause) that he had kept quiet for so long. They enjoyed that, the self-deprecation, the great man's confidence to poke fun at his own reputation for a wordsmith's loquacity, if not garrulity.

'But what did he say in his speech?' Moran's wife asked him in bed later that night.

'I can't remember, Dorothy, I really can't . . . '

'You were there, Charles, for goodness sake, what did he *say*?'

'Listen . . . '

It wasn't what he said, it was the fact that under such pressure, and after a stroke, he could say anything at all. All that mattered was that he had found the words, that was the miracle, the words had returned, that was the relief, and he sent the words into battle. He was into his stride and he didn't flag. He was back where he belonged.

'Fine, but give me some idea of what he said.'

'Oh, all right. He said . . . '

The Prime Minister said . . . something about how he would welcome Germany back to the Great Powers . . . He spoke of NATO and a West German involvement . . . He spoke of a post-Stalin Russia, hoping that by renewed informal contact one good thing might lead to another . . . He hoped we could live in safety with Germany and with Russia . . . They should rejoice that the Korean war was over. But the price of freedom was eternal vigilance . . .

British troops were being sent forthwith to British Guiana in response to threats from the communists ... He looked forward to ever closer ties with the United States, our greatest ally, in the strongest hope that there would never be a third World War ... Housing and denationalisation came up ...

And he hoped Conservative trade unionists would do their best to restrain some of their crackpot union colleagues.

Oh, and he was nice about Anthony.

'That kind of thing, I wasn't really listening in that way.'

'Anthony? Really?'

'Yes.'

'Mentioning Anthony must have been ticklish, that must have been a bit of a moment.'

'I suppose it was.'

As the microphone sent the Prime Minister's words soaring round the Winter Gardens, Margate, Jock Colville occasionally took a quick look away from Winston's speech on his lap to check the reaction of the audience and, in particular, to check the face of Eden. It was pretty clear from a cursory glance that the Foreign Secretary was not enjoying the event one bit. If anything he seemed to be sinking lower and lower in his seat.

And there, to Colville's right, with their notebooks out, were all the newspaper reporters. It was hard for the Prime Minister's secretary to suppress a smile as he watched the whole pack of hacks scribbling away in shorthand, yes, scribble on, preparing to file their stories for the next day's front pages, none of them realising that they had missed the biggest story of all.

Bad luck, chums.

Colville stole a look at his watch. Thirty-nine, forty minutes had passed. The Prime Minister was three-quarters of the way there, more than. A few months before his death Stalin had said that he could think of no other instance in history in which the future of the world depended on the courage of one man alone, as it did in 1940. And that man was the man up on the stage in the Winter Gardens, Margate, the man now speaking and still willing to stand alone.

On that point, if on no other, Stalin was right.

Moran, sitting next to Colville, also looked at his watch. The rest of the steeplechase, he felt, should be easier going. Only a few more hurdles to jump and Winston would be coming down the final furlong with the crowd on its feet, with the grandstand throwing their hats and race cards in the air, roaring him on for one more victory, the greatest racehorse ever, one more victory for a true thoroughbred.

Moran could feel himself almost celebrating, too, ready to throw his own trilby as high as the sky. He could feel his hands begin to unclench and his stomach begin to settle.

No.

Steady on, Charles, not so fast.

Never think you've won the race until you've crossed the

line ahead of the others. It's not over until the referee's final whistle, the final bell, until you've breasted the tape. You could always fall at the final hurdle. Tired old horses, weary from the long race, from being asked to run one long race too many, often did. With all their energy spent, with nothing left, and the going heavy, they slipped or they lost their stride or they hit the hurdle or they misjudged their final leap. Their legs buckled and the crowd gasped and down they went. Not their hearts, rarely their hearts, their hearts were game enough, it was usually their exhausted legs that let them down.

To relax now would be fatal.

Go on, Winston.

Go on!

You're nearly there.

With that impending sense of coming to the end, with the grandstand and the finishing line now in sight, came that modulation and change in his tone, that special moment in his speeches when things became personal. Winston now became very personal. It was one of those moments when it's you and me, heart to heart, voice to voice calling across the deep ocean of humanity.

In the Winter Gardens at Margate on that day, 10 October 1953, you could hear a pin drop.

'And, of course, all of us here, all of us in these islands, rejoice to see Anthony Eden back with us, on his rightful stage. After his grievous illness and long months of strain he is well on the road to full health. No one has done more for this country, served his country more faithfully, in peace and in war. A man unsurpassed to deal with any diplomatic crisis. A man unrivalled in his knowledge of foreign languages and foreign affairs, in which sphere he is quite irreplaceable. Five days ago he selflessly took up once more the reins of his high office. Anthony, we salute you.'

There was warm applause from every section of the hall, an emotional response, a rapport.

What a tribute!

'Consummate,' Jock said to himself, 'a consummate politician.'

Amity, unity, partnership.

Not 'My Right Honourable Friend', not 'the Foreign Secretary', but 'Anthony'. One of us. Eyes, some of them moist, looked in admiration if not awe across to Anthony and then back to the Prime Minister. They were indeed irreplaceable, the Old Man was right, both of them were irreplaceable. One in the Foreign Office, and one at Number 10. The top team, their team, their beloved statesmen, men of the highest calibre and pedigree, men tried and tested in fire, and both still in their rightful places on the world stage.

Winston had been going, had been up on his feet now for forty-seven, forty-eight minutes. The Prime Minister raised his eyes and seemed to peer at the back of the hall. Then he looked down. His chin was on his chest, and appeared to settle there, to have dropped there, almost to be locked there. He took out his large silk handkerchief and slowly wiped his mouth.

There was a long pause.

Moran stiffened.

Clementine panicked.

What was going on? She saw him fumble and try, in a slightly clumsy way, to put his handkerchief back in his breast pocket. Something had gone wrong. He had lost his place. He didn't seem to know what came next. Had there been another arterial spasm? Was he about to blank out, about to make an exhibition of himself? He must sit down!

Her hands started to twitch and her palms to sweat. Her arms hummed and her chest tightened. It felt as if a small electric shock had passed from her heart along her arms and legs and was now running like a current through her fingers and toes. She was on the edge of calling out to Charles and making a scene.

Then the Prime Minister moved a step or two to the table at his side, slowly poured himself a tumbler of water, took a long drink, and, still looking at the water in his glass (pause), said 'I don't often do that.'

The audience roared.

No one could time a line like the old boy.

A flood of relief washed over Clementine, Charles and Jock.

He was all right. He had picked up and he had perked up.

Clementine closed her eyes and thanked God.

But while her eyes were still closed and her mouth was still dry, she heard his voice, his tone, become even more personal, and she knew then for certain that the blow she had dreaded was about to fall.

Knowing him as she did, his point could not have been any clearer. *If I stay on*, he said. If Winston ever began a sentence with *if*, and he used it a number of times, she was quickly on her guard. If he stayed on, if they wished him to stay on, it would not be from any personal ambition but only so that he could help bring about an enduring peace in a troubled world.

Sitting in the middle of the next round of applause Clementine Churchill and Anthony Eden knew, without even a glance, that their hopes and their dreams were, at least for the foreseeable future, to remain unfulfilled. As the Prime Minister started to speak again, the applause died away.

'But, finally, I have something to share with you all. Over the recent summer months, months in which we have seen our most gracious Queen crowned, Mount Everest conquered and the Ashes returned to their rightful place, I have taken the opportunity of the long days of sunlight and the warm evenings, to enjoy all over again some of my favourite works of English literature. The greatest literature in the world.

'In particular I have re-read, even learnt, some of my favourite poems in the comfort of my home in the Kentish countryside. Poems that take me back to my childhood many years ago. Poems that have inspired me during my long life, and poems that have brought me solace or, if needed, stiffened my resolve.

And I leave you today, my friends, with one of them.

'It is by W.E. Henley. Henley was a colourful, larger-than-life character. He could be masterful as well as masterly, bombastic as well as brave, he said what he thought, he lived hard and he played hard, and he was not, it has to be admitted, to everyone's taste. But he took a fair few blows on the chin, he knew adversity as well as triumph and he always came back fighting. It is a well-known poem but, in my view, none the worse for that.'

With a slight tremble in his hands he put his speech down on the lectern and slowly took off his glasses. Then he closed his eyes and slightly raised his chin. After a few moments of silence he began to recite:

Out of the night that covers me
Black as the pit from pole to pole,
I thank whatever gods may be
For my unconquerable soul.

In the fell clutch of circumstance
I have not winced nor cried aloud.
Under the bludgeonings of chance,
My head is bloody, but unbow'd.

Beyond this place of wrath and tears
Looms but the Horror of the shade,
And yet the menace of the years
Finds and shall find me unafraid.

It matters not how strait the gate,
How charged with punishments the scroll,
I am the master of my fate:
I am the captain of my soul.

And that was how he left them.

Then came the first wave.

And during it, Churchill's watery eyes ran uncertainly around, searching out first his life-long darling Clementine, Cat dear, there she was. How was I, Clemmie? You doubted me, be honest, my dear, you did doubt me, didn't you?

Then he could see Colville and Charles. What did you make of that, Charles? Eh, doctor, how did the old carcass do? And Jock, dear sensible Jock, deep down, you were so sensible you weren't sure I could pull it off. You can be too sensible in life, you know, Jock.

In Chartwell, in the dark days of summer, you thought, you all thought I was history; even worse, that I was about to lose. You only saw Singapore falling, while I saw victory in El Alamein. You did, you thought that the auguries were not good, and that I should settle for history and for my place in it. But that was premature because I can still do it. The world still needs me. I am still alive and I rolled the dice, didn't I? I played one more big hand.

The acclaim was now building.

It was building row by row, wave running into wave until there was a great surge, wave after wave of expanding and rebounding sound until they were all up on their feet, some in tears, the whole ecstatic party cheering the Indomitable Old Man, for who he had been, for all he had done in his lifetime, for who he still was and for what he might yet achieve.

Lady Churchill, caught in a swirl, in a vortex of cross-currents, was clapping her gloved hands.

Lord Moran and Jock Colville, standing side by side together in the front row, turned to each other, shook hands and then both went on applauding until their hands hurt.

Rankled, Mr Eden soundlessly tapped his right palm against his left palm.

Sir Winston, with the slightest of puckish grins, bowed his head in modest acknowledgement to the party conference, a packed hall still on its feet, and then he alone sat slowly down. It was as if he was saying, there, that's done. He did not perch on a stool. Nor did he slump down and, above all, he did not flop down from a very great height. To continuing tumultuous thunderous applause he simply and safely resumed his seat.

It was pure Winston.

That was how Jock Colville put it the next morning, and he was right, it was.

*

Nurse Appleyard sat alone in Matron's office. The evening before the Margate speech, Matron had summoned her to say that she could, if she so wished, be released from her duties on the ward while the Prime

Minister's words were being broadcast on the Home Service. The wireless would be left on very quietly. When the speech was over, would she please turn off the wireless and return to her ward.

'Would you like to do that, nurse?'

'Yes, Matron, I would.'

'Then please do. You have done well.'

When the speech was over, Nurse Appleyard sat for a moment or two back at the side of his bed in Chartwell. Then, as she stood upright, she caught a quick glance of herself in the mirror by Matron's desk. She moved a few paces and looked at her face more closely. Perhaps the tiny wrinkles she noticed at the corners of her eyes would go once she'd had a holiday.

Then she turned off the wireless, walked back down the hospital corridors, and returned to her duties.

Author's Note

Sir Winston Churchill served as Prime Minister for seventeen more months before resigning on 5 April 1955 at the age of eighty-one.

Anthony Eden, who succeeded Churchill, was Prime Minister for less than two years, from 1955 to 1957. He resigned on health grounds following the Suez Crisis.

In 1966, fifteen months after Churchill's death, Lord Moran published *Churchill: the Struggle for Survival,* based on the diaries he kept during his time as Churchill's doctor. The Churchill family never forgave him.

Sir John Colville's *The Fringes of Power,* 1985, was partly based on his own diaries, which he kept in a locked drawer in 10 Downing Street, and later edited for publication.

One year later, in 1986, Sir Evelyn Shuckburgh published his diaries under the title *Descent to Suez.*

Reading these diarists greatly helped me and – as is surely the case with anyone who writes a word about Churchill – I am indebted to Sir Martin Gilbert's masterly biographical work.

Nurse Appleyard, I should add, is entirely fictional.

Jonathan Smith,
Southborough, Kent, 2014